HAPPINESS

HAPPINESS

Stories by
MARJORIE AGOSÍN

Translated by
ELIZABETH HORAN

WHITE PINE PRESS · FREDONIA, N.Y.

Translation © 1993 Elizabeth Horan

Acknowledgements:
"Pork Sausages" first appeared in *Américas Magazine*,
"An Immense Black Umbrella" first appeared in *When Angels Glide at Dawn* (Harper Collins, 1991), and "Prairies" and "The Gold Bracelet" first appeared in the *Agni Review*.

This book was published in the original
Spanish by Editorial Cuarto Propio, Santiago, Chile (1991).

Publication of this book was made possible, in part, by grants from the New York State Council on the Arts, the National Endowment for the Arts, and Wellesley College.

Cover Art © 1993 by Heteo Pérez

Book design by Watershed Design

Printed in the United States of America

ISBN 1-877727-34-2

First Edition

9 8 7 6 5 4 3 2 1

Published by
WHITE PINE PRESS
10 Village Square
Fredonia, New York 14063

Translator's Acknowledgements

Amalia Pereira, Guido Heyman, and Diane J. Raynor, and the members of my writing group: Valerie Miner, Julia Douthwaite, and Joan MacGregor, and the late Joseph Silverman, all helped me in developing the ideas I have tried to express in the introduction.

Gabriel Berns offered valuable counsel and lessons on the subtler points of literary translation.

Tomás Montecinos and Carole Michell were endlessly hospitable during a month in their house in Santiago, Chile, where I prepared the earliest draft of this translation. That travel was partially underwritten by Arizona State University grants programs of the Friends of Latin American Studies, Women's Studies, and the College of Liberal Arts and Sciences.

And thanks to my husband, Paul Skilton, who makes possible the bright impossibility, to dwell delicious on.

CONTENTS

INTRODUCTION

HAPPINESS

THE FIESTA

SIGNS OF LOVE

FORESTS

LONG LIVE LIFE

To

Sonia Helena—
  my true happiness

Moises—
  my inspiration

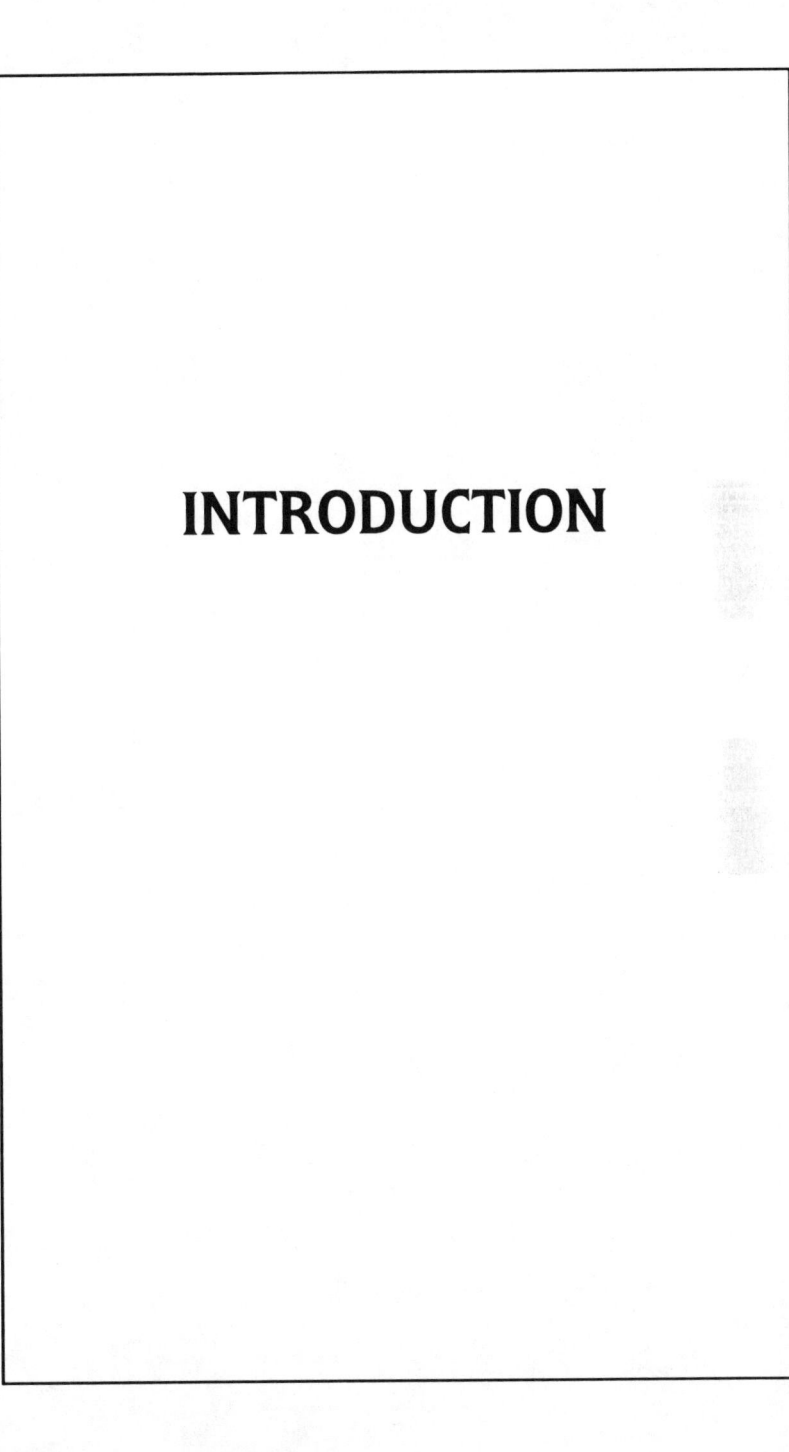

INTRODUCTION

Prelude to a Literary Alliance

In both North and South America, Marjorie Agosín is recognized as one of the most industrious, versatile, and provocative of the generation of Chilean writers now in their thirties. By depicting a world of harshness and illusion, Agosín and her contemporaries challenge the oppressive mediocrity of "light entertainment," aiming instead to disturb us, exposing cultural instability through the depiction of borderline states of consciousness. This aesthetic represents the commitment of a great many Latin American artists to repudiating the complacent, "official" culture fostered by former dictatorships. The alternative exploration of subjectivity reveals truths that bland, "culinary," art-for-consumption tries to hide. Such an approach is as appropriate for readers based in the United States, as for those in Latin America.

Marjorie Agosín's background belies North American stereotypes of Latin Americans. She is the descendant of Russian and Austrian Jews: her great-grandparents fled Odessa and the pogroms, and her Viennese grandparents escaped the Holocaust, emigrating to South America during the early years of the twentieth century. Although Agosín was born in Bethesda, Maryland, her parents returned to their home in Santiago, Chile when she was three months old. For the next sixteen years, she was raised in all the comfort and stability that belonging to Chile's urban middle classes had to offer in the nineteen-sixties: private schools, servants, family vacations. Then, in 1972, the deepening instability of Chile under the Allende regime led Agosín's family to return to the United States. One year later, the military overthrew Chile's democratically-elected government in a bloody coup largely financed by the CIA and initially backed by large segments of Chile's middle classes.

In the years following the 1973 coup, there were mass detentions and summary executions of suspected opponents. The constitution was suspended and the government decreed a massive re-organization of national identity. Many labor leaders, students, and artists who had worked with or had sympathized with the previous government lost their lives. In Chile, as in Argentina, many people were "disappeared," that is, kidnapped and killed for no apparent reason. Many of these people's deaths have yet to be investigated or officially acknowledged, and their bodies have yet to be located, identified, and claimed.

A million Chileans eventually settled outside their country, Marjorie Agosin among them. She attended the University of Georgia, taking a B.A. in Philosophy; in 1982 she received a Ph.D. in Spanish Literature from Indiana University. She has been employed since then as a professor of Spanish at Wellesley College, outside of Boston, where she lives with her husband, John Wiggins, and their two children. Adopting U.S. citizenship has enabled Agosin to work on behalf of the survivors of the disappeared: she could travel to Argentina and Chile and publicize freely their situations without fear of reprisal, and her writing has helped educate an international audience about women's resistance to those dictatorships. Her most recent critical work continues to demonstrate the relation of literature to human rights.

Beyond her four volumes of literary and cultural criticism, Agosin is best known, in the United States, for the several volumes of her poetry that have appeared in bilingual translations. Among Latin American readers, her political work is particularly respected. She has published two documentary collections, *The Mothers of*

Plaza de Mayo and *Scraps of Life: Chilean Arpilleras*. These books recount the stories of women whose family members have been kidnapped, tortured and killed in a systematic campaign designed to wipe out opposition to dictatorship. Those narratives lay the groundwork for the present collection of stories: in her fiction as in her poetry and prose she depicts a wide range of female protagonists who are the historic survivors of persecution and loss.

As with other Latin American Jews, Marjorie Agosín is heir to a complex identity. Consciousness of the Holocaust runs deeper among Chilean Jews, many of whom descend from twentieth century immigrants, than in North American descendants of nineteenth century immigrants. Also, Jews in Chile (20,000 people, or less than a hundredth of one percent in a population of fourteen million) are more markedly a minority than in either the United States or Argentina. The strongly Roman Catholic traditions of Chile make the majority of the population oblivious to religious difference. Organized anti-Semitism may be rare in Chile, but the feeling that the descendants of recent immigrants "aren't really Chilean" is frequent. In Latin American countries with substantial immigrant populations, such as Chile, Argentina, and Brazil, many people think of themselves as Latin American by upbringing or environment only, identifying strongly with European traditions and feeling an affinity for the United States.

Consciousness of such multiple and often conflicting allegiances between religious, national, and ethnic identities has long been central to literature in Spanish. In addition to the questions of immigration and assimilation that many Jewish writers address whatever their language or literary tradition, those seeking to establish a place for themselves within twentieth centuryLatin American literature face a tradition notoriously ambivalent towards multiculturalism. Spain's classic literature documents the tremendous cost, on the individual and national levels, of constructing and feigning racial and religious purity. Travel or emigration to the New World was for centuries prohibitied to anyone suspected of having "Jewish blood". Attempts to create a monoculture by suppressing all multiculturalism singled out generations of Jews and "conversos," the descendants of converted Jews who nonetheless contributed much to the Iberian civilization that forms a common ground among the countries of Latin American. The presence of this tradition makes Agosin's perspective on twentieth century Hispanic multiculturalism both fitting and valuable, as a member of the Jewish minority in Latin America, and of the Spanish-speaking minority in the United States.

My acquaintance with Marjorie has made me feel all the more the importance of conveying for English-speaking readers the political complexity of the development of feminist consciousness in Latin America. Living in Chile, this industrialized and ironic country which enshrined a woman, Gabriela Mistral, as national poet and then ignored her because she was a woman, challenged me to consider how to adapt my North American feminism to a shifting, uncertain Chilean reality. I was struck by what seemed to me a pervasive emphasis in Mistral's writings, among feminists, and in Chile generally, on motherhood as a term women used to characterize women of other classes rather than to describe child-raising. Beyond the stereotype of the working woman from a rural background who heroically labors to support her children despite the opposition of her spouse, I encountered the "woman of means" characterized as lazy (she employs others to care for her children) or frivolous (she delays having children) or selfish (she chooses to pursue a career). I puzzled about how feminism could exist amid such divisiveness and where the ethics of personal independence and "doing-it-yourself" seemed utterly absent. I wondered that Chilean feminists could purchase comfort if not freedom through a class system that assigns nearly all domestic or physical tasks, from serving a meal in a private home to carrying one's groceries, to the category of "servants' work."

I have continued to ask these questions about the effects of work and class on feminism and feminists. When I decided to contact Marjorie Agosin, in the fall of 1988, I knew her as a Chilean poet and feminist who had written intelligently about Gabriela Mistral. thus I knew that through her, these questions would return to my life as if I were again an outsider in Latin America rather than in Boston.

Driving to Marjorie Agosin's house it occurred to me that I had never been to Wellesley before, even though I had spent my entire childhood and most of my adolesence in the nearby town of Canton, some twenty miles distant but worlds away in the caste system of Boston's suburbs. I considered those aspects of daily life in Chile that Boston profoundly lacked: a sense of work and household as continuous, the willingness to pass an afternoon in tea and conversation, the certainty that mutual strangers would have mutual friends.

When Marjorie Agosin and I met, we talked of our mutual friends, of poetry, and of translation. Not long after this she sent me her first story; a few months later, she wrote saying that she was putting together a collection of stories and I agreed to translate the manuscript when she was ready to give it to me. What Marjorie Agosin put onto paper as words that came into her head almost entire, in a kind of dictation, I have similarly sought to bring into English, retaining a sense of their suddenness, their strangeness. The stories in this collection emphasize women as speaking subjects. Sometimes these women's voices appear from the fragments of oral traditions rising out from the surrounding narrative like the roots of a tree poking out from the ground. At other times, that voice produces the narrative all of a piece, naked, unpunctuated, entire, and Marjorie Agosin and I become merely their interpreters.

I have found that the work of the translator, which varies according to culture, shifts many of my questions about Latin American feminism into that cult of the personal and the familiar which shapes all working relationships in Chile, including that of lady and maid. The dynamic can be very like that of writer and editor, of tradition-bearer and folklorist. Because I have been involved with this project from the start, I can retrace the evolution of themes within the collection, from the first packet of some twenty-one stories to the fourth and final batch of ten stories. Among the earlier narratives, the reconstruction of a historical past predominated;

among the later ones, the exploration of erotic subjectivity. Individually and as a whole they describe a continuing metamorphosis in the contexts of travel and emigration, of sexual encounters, or urban survival in tenuous circumstances.

Agosin says that she writes from the perspective of Chile's middle class. This is a perspective that readers in the United States may not ordinarily associate with Latin America or with Chile, where the term "middle class" is used very broadly. From factory workers and garage mechanics to wealthy businessmen and luxury-loving travellers, virtually every Chilean I have met has claimed to be of the middle class. Belonging to the Chilean middle classes consists more of customs observed rather than the control of capital: so important is the ritual of "going on vacation," for instance, that people will close up their houses in Santiago so that their friends and neighbors think that they have gone on vacation while they continue living there. This bourgeois concern with appearances is part of what fascinates me about Chile and reminds me of my own childhood, in the early sixties, in suburban Boston: the long vanished ethic of sin or salvation is replaced by "What will the neighbors think?"

Like Chilean fiction writers María Luisa Bombal and José Donoso, Agosin mocks the pretensions of good family, good manners, and good money on which the class system depends. Where U.S. writers are often content with revealing the "hollowness" of a life dictated by routine, these Chilean writers concentrate on an alternative reality dominated by dreams, and the shape of things lost. Access to that world is often controlled by servants or by a return to "magical" sites such as forests and deserted beaches. As with other experimental writers in Latin America, identity is revealed in actions and their consequences. Questions of whether the torturers are Argentine, Chilean, Salvadoran, for example, or from what family or class background, are irrelevant to Agosin. She addresses larger questions of politics, ethics, and history: how to live as a survivor, how to remember and mourn the dead, what are the conditions of love and surrender, what are the possibilities of eroticism in otherwise quotidian encounters.

Agosin also draws from and adds to a tradition of writing by women that dates back several generations in Chile. Short fiction based in part on mundane experience and in part on the riotous life of the imagination has roots in the cosmopolitan fictions of María Luisa Bombal, in the reminiscences of Inéz Echeverría, in the creative efforts of salonnières such as Sara Hubner. She shares with Gabriela Mistral and other poets who experimented with prose (Pedro Prado, Eduardo Barrios) similarities and affinities with French writers such as Baudelaire and Rimbaud: they concentrate on the evocative power of the image as opposed to the literary naturalism of the late nineteenth century novel. In part, this tradition of prose poetry has made Latin America writers and audiences especially receptive to surrealism and to the mixing of genres. But largely it is the constant presence of unlikely juxtapositions, improbable histories, and day-to-day absurdities in Latin American that makes it impossible, as Garcia Marquez has pointed out, to create "pure" fiction, or even to recognize fiction as distinct from history or journalism.

For all of these influences, the collaboration that produced this collection of tales sets it apart from the preceeding literary traditions. I liken the circumstances to the situation that resulted in the stories known as *The Thousand and One Nights,* a collection of tales told by Scheherazade, the bride of a deranged Sultan. After having been deceived by his first wife, to whom he had been devoted, the Sultan wed anew each day in order to have his bride executed on the next. Scheherazade told stories morning and night to delay the order of execution that awaited her. What is less known about Scheherazade is that she had a collaborator, her sister Dinarzade, and that the two women worked together on behalf of the other women in the realm. Their father was the man charged with providing the Sultan with new wives and killing the old ones, so he was horrified when his daughter Scheherazade wanted to marry the Sultan. He begged her not to, but Scheherazade was stubborn; she had her way. Scheherazade requested only that her sister, Dinarzade, be allowed to share her bedchamber for what would be their last night together. In the plan that the two women worked out, Dinarzade was to wake her sister an hour before daybreak, saying, "My dear sister, if you are not asleep, tell me I pray you, before the sun rises, one of your charming stories. It is the last time that I shall have the pleasure of hearing you."

The stories that Scheherazade tells are not, properly speaking, "hers," and they do not belong to anyone, really: they are tales that she repeats as she had heard them told, or imagined in the words of another. Dinarzade's agency is even more ambiguous: she joins in instigating the stories, that is, in bringing them out, ensuring that they have a public. Dinarzade may just be fulfilling the requirements of the situation: that there be someone to awaken the teller and ask for a story. She may be acting out of loyalty to her sister, or she may know that her sister's life depends on it. She may even have encouraged Scheherazade to marry the Sultan in the first place, trusting in her sister's ability to entertain and knowing that as long as she lives, the Sultan will forget his plans to execute a woman a day.

Dinarzade may have joined her sister in a spirit of loyalty compounded with self-interest, or either of these: if the stories weren't told, the killing would go on, and someday it would be her own turn to face the executioner. The two sisters are caught up in a collaboration for motives inextricably linked with the circumstances in which that telling occurs, be it the specifics of the delayed execution or the wider context of the culture that sanctions those murders and makes it necessary for women to join together, to save other women under the guise of providing entertainment.

Marjorie Agosin expresses the faith that "if a story is good, it will find a hearer," but I think of the person who brings the story to life by hearing it, who takes down a testimony and invariably edits it, and of how that task of taking down dictation resembles not only the translator's, but the writer's task. The translator and writer are engaged in essentially the same action, each one trying to locate the voice in the text, to shape a meaning out of the infinite possibilities of words. The individual author cum creative genius, wholly responsible for executing composition and controlling all variants, does not exist. Fictions brought across cultures especially indicate how author-ity derives from collaborative activity. This is most vividly illustrated in the case of testimonies and oral histories, genres that in Latin American literature have been vital for bringing recognition to otherwise marginalized or silenced persons. The woman who can write and has access to the tape recorder, the typewriter, or the press, records the stories of those who are supposedly without voice: the story belongs to all of its tellers and listeners.

There will always be some readers wanting to romanticize the artist as an especially intuitive soul who is so much better or more sensitive, more important than we are. The danger of this view is that it mystifies the circumstances in which texts are actually produced: it encourages passive "appreciation" on the part of readers, rather than asking them to consider what they get out of, and put into, their pleasure in reading. Rather than look to the artist, then, let us look to the figures who people them, to the trees and beaches, to the avenues, to the nights and mornings, the scenes of stories that become the shape of the present landscape of sea, rocks, snow and flowers. If we live in the stories, we become part of that world. Sharing stories about lands and people we have known can bring them back from oblivion, restore them. This art of sharing stories knows how to take the tormenting visions and the dream of sunflowers, to just paint it and leave it hanging, in the air of the page, just past the trace of the intervening hand. It is through such stories that the valuable testimony of the dead comes to us, guiding us, if we let them speak, if we wait for them, if we prepare ourselves to receive their dictation. It is not too much to receive them, although they may be intolerant of interruption, vain and jealous in their need to be written, to be read. After all is said, reading returns the spoken word to life.

The first of the stories that Marjorie Agosin sent me appears here under the title "Prairies." It explores her family history of flight and persecution, bringing that history into the present by recounting a strange, almost hallucinatory encounter in the United States

Midwest, between two descendants of Austrians, one a Jewish woman from Chile, the other, a woman whose parents worked in the concentration camp at Auschwitz. This story illustrates how the continuing presence of the past dictates who these two women are and how they see one another. The consciousness of Europe brings with it mixed emotions for both women. That story, like "Adelina," conveys a sense of how Latin America and Chile were to have been a kind of promised land, an escape from religious, political persecution and the threat of detention.

By putting the theme of the disappeared into the context of historical persecutions generally, Agosin indicates that it is no accident that those who have worked on behalf of the friends and relatives of the detained, trying to determine the whereabouts of their bodies, trying to learn something of the circumstances of their deaths, take as their slogan, "never again." The return to unmarked gravesites in Pisagua, Chile, like the return to the meadows of Austria, illustrates a powerful theme in Agosin's work: the continuing presence of the dead, who return from land or sea to bury the living.

The title piece, "Happiness," is ironic: it is the story of a woman's revenge on false friends whose friendship turns to rage because they cannot stand the thought of being abandoned. While they calculate the destruction of her reputation through malevolent gossip, she determines to undo them through a perfectly planned feast executed as only one who has known a similar gourmandise could. In "Happiness" as in "Emma" we wonder what friendship between women can be about, given the examples of mothers who warn that promises of intimacy between women, especially with "the urgently ladies," are wholly conditioned on reciprocal favors, and that such women regard true love as a betrayal and an opportunity for gossip. Since intimacy between women is central to many of these stories, a lack of intimacy can be very disturbing, especially when the divisive effects of class are everywhere apparent

Latin America feminists, as opposed to many of their U.S. counterparts, seem far more aware of how class allegiance enters into the construction of female identity. The individual woman who regards herself as a good mother, an upstanding housekeeper, a sexy bed-partner, develops that self-image out of a complex network of oppositions. Perhaps as a consequence of having lived so long in the United States, Agosin can look critically at the elements of day-to-day life that many a woman of privilege in Latin America might take as her due. The first story in this collection, "Slaves," satirizes some of the preoccupations, the self-consciousness that the category of the "good woman," united with privilege, produces: an obsession with cleanliness and subsequent horror of the body. The narrator is vaguely aware that her "superiority" is constructed entirely out of things that she pays another woman to do for her. This elite woman is so terrified at the very possibility of her maid's being capable of speech that she completely monopolizes the conversation; terror creates a similarly harrowing monologue of domestic disenchantment in "The Hen." In "Slaves," the strongest interdictions aim at preventing speech, such as the "two inflamed tales" of the servant's hands uncovering the jewelry chest, or the dangerous magic of the servant's resentment expressed through curses she mutters while watering the plants.

The reverse of the view satirized in "Slaves" appears in the story "An Immense Black Umbrella." Here, "the servant question" is viewed retrospectively, almost with a kind of nostalgia, as the narrator describes her gradual realization that while the woman, Delfina Nahuenhual, who raised her, was at the center of her childhood world, she knew nothing, really, of that woman's feelings. Even after she is chosen to be the bearer of that woman's writings, she has no clue to their meaning or even their destination, for this is information that Delfina Nahuenhual sees no reason to share with someone who is, after all, only a girl that she took care of after she nearly lost her own life in a momentous earthquake. Similarly, in the story "Nana," the narrator knows that the woman she hires to take care of her son sits in judgment on her: each regards the other as an evil spirit. The narrator has only the power to dismiss her and so she does, suspecting this mysterious woman of having caused not only her miscarriages but those of her mother whom the woman had also served. If there is any escaping the cycle of resentment and guilt, having the housekeeper "sent back" is only a stop-gap solution to the struggle that the narrator sees as based in the bestowal or refusal of love.

To take seriously the exaltation of a feminine intuition based in the body means also taking on all of the frailties to which that body is heir. This core of Agosin's interest in female identity is manifest in nostalgic eroticism, as in "Distant Root of Autumn Loves." Again and again the stories return to this question of the body: in looking for the bodies of dead lovers or sons, in encountering the evidence of mortality, in heterosexual love, and in adorning rites that assert a precarious, isolated, femininity. In "Happiness," in "Blood" and "Blood II," in "Beds," and in "The Dead," the desire for and experience of corporeal motherhood is presented as a means of transformation, for women to achieve a subjectivity centered not on limitations but on possibilities. Thus in "Happiness" the narrator's former companions regard her preference for her husband and son as a betrayal of the self-indulgent life that she once shared with them. The narrator's decision to strike back is triggered by the desire to protect her good name. Ironically, she engineers her revenge by taking these most "unwomanly women" captive in her home while she escapes.

In other stories that criticize women's virtual enslavement to the idea of love, "village commentary," that is, the power of others to create or destroy one's reputation, often figures in. There's Guillermina in "The Fiesta" who dreams of being swept off her feet, and Teresa, the butcher's wife in the story "Fat," whose passivity and acquiescence are so extreme that her willingness to become a mute vehicle for the butcher's desire becomes a subject of scandal. In the meantime, her own speech is completely suppressed, turned into signs, such as "her strange upturned hands." As in the story "Braids," beauty is disfigured by becoming a figure in the dreams of others. In "Braids," however, the central character's decision to reject the beauty of her hair ultimately becomes an obsession for her, turning her into a Frankenstein of the beauty parlors.

One of the defining characteristics of female subjectivity in these stories is a response to loss by turning inward. Finding that no one remains to take care of us as childhood grows ever more distant, we are left somehow to fend for ourselves. If we survive, that pain provides the foundation for a new identity, although many of the women described here remain mute. The focus on corporeal experience leads not just to the contemplation of connections and disconnections (described in the two sections of "Blood"). In a modern world that has few ceremonies for commemorating loss; the stories "Mirrors," "Monserrat Ordoñez" and "Sargassos" show how women have precious little evidence to verify that they have even existed. Yet the future can be transformed through caresses, through gestures of love written in the palms, through the caressing hands of women like Gloria Landaeta, witch #77 in the story "Gypsy Women."

Agosin, like many women writers, looks to childhood in an attempt to restore the loss of autonomy that the mother, the housewife, the lover all experience in these stories. Childhood presents a topic of great potential power in part because the voice of the child, reconstructed nostalgically, can be the voice of command. Further, the young girls in these stories live with the promise of transformation, as expressed, for instance, in a visit to Easter Island, in "An Immense Black Umbrella."

Enlisting the perspective of a child restores the strangeness of a time when nothing made sense except according to the simplest explanations. It is the perspective of a child, then, in "Orphanages," that complains about the barbarity of the customs surrounding death in the United States, where rather than crying the guests all stand around exclaiming how lovely the makeup job is. In "Emma" the narrator is a child in that she accepts only story-book transformations: although everyone says that Emma had to move because her father was "disappeared," she knows that Emma is waiting for her and knows her thoughts, since they are "soulmates." Or in the story "Pork Sausages," the narrator recalls her love-affair as a very young girl with a man much older than she. Her greatest pleasure was in the fact of its being forbidden and secret, unfortunately broken apart by a wicked, broom-wielding woman named Menchu who seemingly devotes her existence to spoiling their innocent, guilty "fun."

Many of the characters described her live lives that seem almost foreordained, through world events and their own personal peculiarities, to encounter an end that is but a strange variation on where they began. Such is the case in "The Seamstress from Saint Petersberg." The seamstress's needles and brocades create miraculous blouses for the czarina; she narrowly escapes the pogrom carrying only a needle and thimble, and she finds her way to London where she maintains that identity. In the end as in the beginning, the czarina spots her and bestows favor. In the story "Photographs," a woman drawn to document freak shows, street fights, and prostitutes has the heavy door of her family's vast bourgeois house forever closed to her as a result of her fascination. Choosing to live on the edges of a world that her parent's wealth tries to shut out she learns how to survive on her own, finding that the gift for discerning hidden truths and disasters brings her the deepest knowledge of who she is in relation to her family.

It is not the machinery of plot but the combination of feeling and precisely described states of consciousness that carry these narratives. The narrator trusts to our curiosity about how this world came to exist, where it is, and its relation to our own world, to make the stories reveal themselves as the unfolding of a mysterious event. The terms "magical realism" and "literature of the fantastic," frequently and ambiguously applied to fiction that somehow represents some of the worlds that make up Latin America, is hopelessly inadequate to the complex relations of gender and power represented herein. In these accounts of triumph despite adversity are women who have survived by their wits and a certain consciousness of destiny brought by the knowledge of other women's lives.

—Elizabeth Horan
Department of English
Arizona State University

HAPPINESS

SLAVES

And after you've closed that front door for the fourth time remember to pass a slightly damp but well-wrung rag over the mahogany threshold and also remember to shine the doorbell, then come into the main rooms barefoot and, with the utmost care and caution, start dusting my collection of porcelain shoes, and don't forget the trouble you'll be in should you break them. Remember they were brought over in ships as cargo by slaves much like you, although you're not really a slave since you can go out for a day and a half every third month and what's more you've a roof over your head and a blanket. Yesterday I inspected your room and what a fright that was, the braids that you weave from witches' wool and I saw that you had hung nets from crystals smeared with blood. Once you've finished with the shoes, go over to the china collection. Remember that each plate must be minutely scraped, strip it with all that scrubbing, with your crafty Indian's hands. Also, water some of the plants, but I forbid you to repeat those curses in those strange languages that sound like spirits and bad noises. Then, after many hours, after the night makes a well of wounds in your dark face, head for the bedrooms. Take excellent care of the sheets of good people like us, sheets without semen, sheets without wrinkles, and, on that account, take care not to cause the sheets to have the slightest wrinkle and don't forget, I repeat, *do not forget to* clean the cracks in the windows and to kill the unfortunate untimely pigeons that would have fearlessly stayed in that room where the motions of love are ceremoniously practiced, those motions different from yours, not with open fearful legs sweating, as if you had dug into the earth and were drooling, because they say that when you stop wallowing around in the mosses you give thanks to the earth for showing favor, but good women like us know why the sheets must always be stretched tight, letting no wrinkles enter our bodies, whereas you make perverse offerings of your bed, altars, and I can do nothing but look at you with anger or in fear. Then don't forget that you must sweep the room in thousands of directions beginning with the corners where the sweat accumulates, returning along the right where you begin traipsing in circles as if practicing an intense rhythm, and then returning to go over the sheets, stretching them tight and scrubbing out the stains, though you know quite well that good people like us are incapable of staining them; still, I insist that you must clean everything with a routine mandated by impeccable training in the domestic arts, and don't forget that you must attend to the geometry of the furniture—I was forgetting about that—and you must brush my mahogany jewel box but never open it up because your hands would become two inflamed tales. Then, when you finish the bedrooms go to the bathrooms where you must iron my hand towels and the towel with which I pat my secret parts, and you must be very careful that your odor never gets mixed up with mine because you smell like a poor chlorinated Indian. Then, after you finish cleaning the towels, shine the racks meticulously and also take care with the tiny wrinkles the towels might get and be sure afterwards to devote yourself to picking strands of my golden hair from the hairbrush, and if you wish I might permit you to keep a few so they will say that you worked in my household and that you were treated like a queen and that there were even times when you were given a bit of salt—although I never understood why one night when it was darker than your seeds I saw you sprinkling sea salt around the doorways—and now that I have given you these instructions go out and change your apron that's as green as the cilantro or those herbs that you strangely kiss and keep in your percale skirts and now give me a glass of water because that's true charity but before you do comb me out, arrange my hair so that I don't look like you, bring me my glasses—*I* know how to read—but before you do, mix me a vodka with ice and don't let it occur to you to poison me or ever put salt in the drinks of people like us.

HAPPINESS

Happiness, for those women, did not consist of petting cats or gazing at sunsets from a yellow sailboat. Nor did it consist of caressing their husbands and little children. Happiness for them consisted of boiling potatoes in order to devour them, strangling chickens along the beach to savor the very instant of death. After indulging that taste, with an air of vain satisfaction their stomachs would stealthily grow with the slices of dead meat which placidly lay in the immense cavities of their bellies.

At first they liked me because I went along with them in the sacred rites of their feasts. I didn't share their taste for things that had rotted or for hot, raw, crimson flesh, but I did like the cheeses from Argentine cows and the French fries. Even so, I couldn't always finish my pieces of cheese or delicate fritters, magnificent for the double dose of chloresterol, for they would hurl themselves at my plate, they would go crazy eating the last French fry, and they'd smile, Mafia-like and deeply moved.

When they launched into my plate, into the caresses of my husband, when they began arriving at the stroke of midnight or at dawn in search of some slices of smoked ham or onions or dried chili peppers, I started to hate them. No longer could I bear to go on at all hours in gluttonous rites. No longer could I bear to hear them speak of women condemned to thinness. I wanted to make poems and children. I was interested in writing a book about the transmigration of meals from the New World to the Old, in giving talks about corn, and I wanted no more of them.

They began to talk against me when I hemorrhaged and lost two children. I could see that they were fascinated with my sadness. I never thought they were evil, but something in me rejected them like spoiled meat.

Over the months they started yelling at me in the middle of the street. They threatened me and invented slanders, they accused me of eating neither lamb nor ham. They noted my being Jewish. They accused me of not attending witches' sabbaths with lard-lobsters, fried eggs and oily juices. For years I had to put up with them, until the arrival of my first-born son, who filled my belly with life, with colors, and not with fermented sausages.

With my son, my happiness really began, along with deep suffering for them. I was so happy talking to him and telling him poems—with or without rhymes. I was happy kissing his little fingernails and ears and for months I contemplated him as if in a fantasy. I stopped eating and sleeping only to smell him. I was so wildly happy.

It was my happiness that those women could not pardon. My thinness they had already accepted but not my happiness. They attacked me in the early mornings, sending me greasy knives. They sent me letters written on napkins and pieces of long-dead fish. I did not respond to their tactics, but I secretly wanted to poison them, to distance them from my life for some hours. Why didn't I tell them "Forever"?

One afternoon I invited them to a big party, planned for them alone, so that I could give them my undivided attention. I made a tablecloth of greens so they could eat that immediately, if they wanted. From Peru came some fifty-two varieties of potato, from Costa Rica the entire banana production of the last decades, and Argentine cows, of course—the ones that weren't starving just yet.

My house was lit with candles and immense lanterns that resembled the texture of their arms. They had scarcely opened their mouths when the tablecloth was swallowed up along with the strawberry-shaped paper cups. Then the Venetian blinds and cellophane disappeared. They ate like crazy, in love with their own fastidiousness and gluttony.

Once they grew drowsy and the rich streams of food descended into their shredded stockings, I brought out the cheesecake. They insisted that they were too full and couldn't try it, but I insisted with the gentleness that cruel people have. When they ate the first mouthful, they emitted moans of love and feverishly continued, madly devouring the ricotta that squeezed out from between their fingers. The more the cheesecake shrank, the more they grew and grew. They were all puffed up, and I was concerned about the roof of my house because they would not fit through the door. They became so puffed up that they drifted up toward the ceiling. They begged me to help them get down. Shouting, they promised that they would never slander me again. They pledged power and eternal love for me.

Smiling, I called the fire department to take them away, and I went off looking for some soup with which to enjoy my liberty. When the firemen finally arrived, the women were so fat that no one could bring them to earth. For years they remained elevated without even a mouthful of food, until they became some sad, famished fat women. My desire to poison them diminished and now that they had come back to earth, they calmed down and thanked me for helping them lose weight and recover their souls.

FAT

Watching herself with the eyes of a wounded and terrified bird, she is lost and does not stop watching her hands, hands that have taken on the color of wounded things, and at times when she seems to be contemplating her hand, she strips naked, as if she were drunkenly looking at the outline of hands that have already lost their lines and crossroads, hands that caress the butcher with a crazed rapidity, hands that make things by habit and out of duty, and each day she closes in on the lands of exile, the landscapes of darkness, and the townspeople tell her that every morning she becomes more and more ugly, perhaps on account of the cursed butcher who makes her spend hours turning the fat, that thick fat, perverse, that fat which resembles dreams of lingering death, and there is Teresa so beautifully ugly with her turned-up hands, with her humble rebellious face and her hands turning around and around in the color of burnt things, and the butcher, when he went crazy, asking her to undress next to the fat because his heart was trembling and it was so infinitely sweet to him, to feel her breath layered and greasy alongside the dead meat, and on days when meat is prohibited he asks that she not stop stirring the pots in the backroom, he asks that she not stop smelling of fat, that she not stop at stirring it, and that she anoint her body with his messages, with his aches and pains and I think — we all think — about Teresita looking at herself in filth, contemplating herself in the transitory madness of her legs, her glances full of silence and not even loving the things of the flesh, not even an unclothed body of utmost beauty to contemplate and, in contemplation, to shape the surface of their desires.

Everybody says that Teresa started getting really ugly when she married the butcher and began devoting herself to stirring immense vats of fat that resemble dry springs, the dead coals of wrath, and at times Teresa asks that they give her a chicken, that she might have a bird so its head will stretch toward the sky far from the stupor of the fat.

BRAIDS

For María Luisa Bombal

Her flourishing, illuminated hair was a dense braid where birds built nests. Her parents combed it sometimes, inventing birds, valleys and villages that resembled her complexion's smoothness. The light passed through her undulating mane and many men from the town dreamed of her naked, covered only by that thickness that at times seemed a great forest. But she never stroked her hair, and she chose hollow mirrors that disfigured and cut short the breath of her immense and intemperate mane. She spent hours combing dolls until their tresses fell out, and she kept their shorn scalps alongside the remaining strands that fell from her hands.

She collected dolls with the calm perseverance of those who keep secrets in the silence of dark rooms, cutting through the darkness as mistress of herself and of the priceless skulls in her doll collection.

She went about wearing her hair in mourning after her early childhood; she bound it in a very thin, somewhat bone-colored handkerchief, and she liked talking of the bristling hair of night and of evil times. Everyone desired her, past those far-off gestures, past that glance which controlled the landscape of her hair.

Those who loved her wound up avoiding her, since she did not permit them to cover the crown of her head with caresses; instead it remained covered with that invincible handkerchief which day by day grew more like the color of bones and of escape. Because nobody loved her, she chose the complaints of love. She went sweeping stray hair from the hateful beauty parlours in stubborn local neighborhoods that she entered during the most intimate hollow of night. She gathered the hair of old women, of sickly brides, of wives, of cutthroats, keeping it in the most intimate corner of her own handkerchief that began to swell like a river, a tumor, and she continued going insane, tearing away at the hair gathered from the floor.

But nothing could satisfy her greed. Her gestures increasingly possessed the distance of invalids. Then, on her own, she decided to pull hair from the scalps of the devout clients. She prepared for them a brew of smoke and smooth fragrances, putting them to sleep early, so sweetly, leaving them stitched into the fullness of sleep. Then, she bitterly began tugging first at the ringlets, then at the side-locks that embraced the faces of the walk-in customers. And in the tremendous angry and savage silence of the hair salons, she made them very much her own. On waking, the women felt bald and unloved. It was useless to yell, because they lay silenced, shrouded in their colored robes. Every day she seemed to wrap herself more in a pelt of fur, similar to the tattooing of hyenas on the nights of the dead.

Thus she became helpless, strange, wrapped in dead roots, in the shrouds of exile because she never was able to cut a dead woman's hair, because she believed and she lived and, full of envy, she never managed to satisfy her last wish: to cut her own hair.

AN IMMENSE
BLACK UMBRELLA

When she arrived at our house she was covered by an immense black umbrella and a blindingly white gardenia hung from her left ear. My sister Cynthia and I were between hallucination and fear, looking at her. Now I think that there was also something in her that invited a nostalgia for the remote, the lost, the inevitably sad. Back then she seemed like an enormous fish or a woman who had been shipwrecked, out of place, including that umbrella that had nothing to do with rain, since it possessed various orifices where even the hint of water would've leaked through, in that surprising dry summer, a summer in which my sister and I learned the reason for magical things such as the arrival of Delfina Nahuenhual.

My mother approached to greet her and she brazenly answered with a toss of her head that she always travelled accompanied by that enormous umbrella to protect herself from the sun, from the spirits, and from little girls like us. A smile emerged from my mother's elegant lips and from then on the two of them were partners in crime rather than "lady" or "servant."

Delfina Nahuenhual (since that's what she said she should be called, by her full name) was one of the few survivors of the earthquake in Chillán, in the south of Chile. She lost children, houses, her wedding dress, hens, and two favorite lemon trees. She was able to rescue only that enormous black umbrella, which gave off an odor of rubble and neglect.

At night she used to light a brazier that emitted some very sweet, fine flames, and she would wrap herself in an enormous shawl of blue wool that didn't scratch, and she always wore pieces of potato on her temples to ward off bodily infirmities and cold drafts. On having begun the night's rituals, Delfina Nahuenhual would tell stories of frogs turned into princes and of souls in torment. Little by little her generous lap would put us to sleep and half-awake, half-dreaming, her voice let us dream the dreams of children put to rest in learning the gestures, the ceremonies of love. By the time that we were nearly asleep Delfina Nahuenhual would get to work writing very long letters that she then doubled by wrapping them in newspaper. She kept the letters in a battered old pot where she also collected garlic cloves, cilantro, and sprigs of parsley.

My sister and I, who loved her to distraction, tried our hardest to examine the contents of those letters, as well as the addressee's place of residence, and when Delfina Nahuenhual enveloped herself in the odors of her adored stove, we climbed up to where the pot was to discover that secret which was part of our obsessions.

Our attempts to read the missives failed miserably. Cynthia and I returned, shame-faced, to our bed while Delfina Nahuenhual smiled at us and pushed us away with her broom.

For many years we continued with the ceremonies of the stories alongside the fire. My brother Mario was born, the family favorite, and Delfina Nahuenhual would sit him on her generous knees and thus he too heard that once upon a time there was a prince who long ago had been a frog, just as he also observed, hallucinatory, how that pot where the letters were kept was stuffed not only with letters but also with garlic braids to ward off envy.

Delfina Nahuenhual, on a warm morning much like the one when she had arrived, told us that she was tired, that she needed to return to the South where she had some small savings and a cow, enough to get by in peace. I thought that she was looking forward to dying by rising up to the sky and because of this, she had decided to return to her mosses and her clay pots.

When she bid us goodbye, I can remember only having cried a great deal. My brother Mario clung to her enormous skirts; he was seeking the wisdom of a woman who was never a servant to us. When she approached to kiss me she told me that some day I should deliver the letters to their addressee but that I should keep the old pot.

For many years I watched over her little pot as I would a valuable secret, a kind of magic lantern in which I was hoarding my childhood. When I wanted to remember her, I'd rub the little pot, it would give off a smell, and all fears would vanish along with the darkness.

With her departure I came to understand that all of childhood had gone with her and now more than ever I miss New Year's, the dishes of lentils she'd prepare for good luck and prosperity. I long for her skin, her smell and those tales that I remember all the more because I remember her expressions and her love.

My sister Cynthia had her first daughter. Mario went abroad. I decided to honeymoon on Easter Island since those immense strange statues had seduced me ever since I was very little. They seemed to have appeared at the threshold of the earth in some mysterious magic way, like the arrival of Delfina Nahuenhual and her enormous black umbrella. I carried with me the letters that I'd moved from the pot to an enormous moss-green trunk, carefully preserving the few cloves of garlic that still remained. As an adult I was never tempted by curiosity to read the letters. I knew only that they must be delivered.

One morning when the sun lit even the most hidden corners I approached the indicated address: a leper-colony, one of the few that exist on this planet. A business-like official opened the door and quickly accepted the packet of more or less 500 letters. I asked if the addressee was living and he said yes of course but any meeting was impossible; he couldn't be seen. When I handed them over I seemed to have lost one of my most valuable possessions, perhaps the last scraps of life of my Delfina Nahuenhual.

I never learned who Delfina Nahuenhual wrote these letters

for, nor how she spent her sleepless nights thinking about them, dreaming them up, only that their addressee was a leper on Easter Island, still alive and perhaps reading every night the letters, the dreams, of Delfina Nahuenhual. When I returned to the hotel I thought that those letters had not met their fate by chance. Then I looked at the sky as she had taught us and an immense black umbrella covered the thick clouds.

ADELINA

Emma Weiss had never seen the sea, although she imagined that it was copper-colored like the untamable hair of her Viennese ancestor,s and of her mother, Frida Weiss, who wore it bundled up, tied in a blue loop as if the knotted secrets of her wanderings and rivals were guarded within. The sea always looked like an unfathomable horizon, or like her dreams, like music from the bottom of the water that Emma Weiss invented every evening in the remote landscapes of Osorno, Chile, where the silence and the obscurity of the meadows swarmed, and the whistling of the animals predicted change and the births of children and trees.

Her father had escaped long before the tattoos of war. They say that he had done so through an act of love and faith. In love with an exquisite and brave cabaret singer who worked in the all-night districts of the city, he had decided, once and for all, to declare an end to this illicit love. In the month of June, when it was possible to walk about in free air and the incomprehensible smell of wildflowers filled the fullness of the air, Joseph Weiss decided to sprout from the last corner of Vienna and go to Valparaíso, city of ports and sun-lit hills. Thus, he bid goodbye, fearful, to Adelina, to her swift legs and spangled suit, because he foresaw, through her maddening habits, her insinuating and defeated wrinkles, the beginnings of the crash, the senseless bombardments and the indisputable failure of all menace and war. They said goodbye in the plaza with the certainty of those who remain loving one another, near to the earth and to the curve of kisses. They even chose the festivity of the place, where entire families were frolicking, as if they were immortal, because sunshine and children played on the old wooden benches.

Emma Weiss prepared herself for the trip to Valparaíso, and for the first time she would come close to smelling the sea, to seeing its swell and its mystery for all its splendor and delirium. Emma Weiss would also meet her grandmother, Elena, who had remained closed up in the cellar of the house of Adelina, because she was the mother of José Weiss, because she was Jewish. One had to watch out in the city, to circle around the streets before heading for the cellar, to take note very early in the morning that no one was observing. Adelina was liable to enter on the sly, offering peace and her smile delivered as a sustenance into Elena's slender hands. Together, the two women remembered José Weiss and they closed the shutters to light a candle, to illuminate the dead souls and to remember that Jewish navigator who arrived like a soul in trial, descending from the deepest part of his strangled destiny to the strange skirts of Valparaíso with a child of a few months in his arms.

The night before the trip on the train from Osorno to Valparaíso, Emma Weiss ironed her violet linen dress, she brushed her thick, sober hair over and over and again she dreamed of her grandmother Elena and of the sea. She desired it with the innocence of first things, as when she looked at herself naked under the shutters of her room and became beautiful in a dawning roundness. She imagined herself bathed in the sea, letting the water fill her with life and people her with seaweed, and she slept as if the sea had entered her eyes, as if the stories of terror, of the children sent away on the trains of dementia, had been buried in the very cortex of the gulfweed.

In the train they travelled through enormous pastures, past humble, defeated animals, and the smell of smoke impregnating the landscape no longer reminded them of a Europe split in two, for they were rescued in time, thanks to the love of Adelina, who permitted

José Weiss to arrive on the Chilean coast before he received a detention order.

Emma Weiss' hands were sweating. It seemed a day of false summer. She rarely glanced at her father who still wore his hat from Vienna and the look of Adelina in his deep green eyes.

The port seemed disorderly, as if God or the constant earthquakes had deliberately forgotten to assemble Valparaíso and the port, and the city seemed rather like a cord of unruly, combed hair and the hills were the size of the people. Maybe that's why it didn't seem strange when Emma Weiss saw a coffin coming down a hill or a bride running over the stony ground.

The day was an intense blue and the sky mingled with the sea. Emma Weiss had already spied the ship on which her grandmother, Elena, whom she had never seen, would arrive. Meanwhile Elena, in the ship, could not stop remembering when she herself, with the intuition of a clairvoyant, had urged Joseph to leave. Kissing him on the hair in silence, she had offered a blessing for the traveller. But José Weiss was thinking of Adelina in the shiny blouse that she would put on in the fatal nights, before the specters of death and of bombs that seemed like black doves swathed in feathers of bad luck.

The hands of Emma Weiss were sweating; she loosened the violet bow and her hair more and more resembled copper-colored algae. Someone tossed paper streamers and she timidly threw a few of them into the sea, thinking they might fall in her grandmother's hair. And there was the pious sea, receiving the emigrants, pressing on their boat and the padlocks of their souls, while Emma already belonged to the sea, for she had dreamed that her body was a cradle of fish in its lap. Then, suddenly, José saw Elena Weiss. There she was coming with her same tulle hat, smaller, thin-faced, her hair carrying the memory of many deaths. But she understood that she had chosen to live and she saw Joseph with his summer smile too and his eyes like the forests.

The anxious families tossed paper streamers. Others played little crinkled paper horns that resonated with the splendor of the sloping hills and someone saw from afar a bride dancing along the summits. Valparaíso was strange, perched as if on wings and crazy in its sanity while the sailors streamed out from the ship along with people who were bidding love goodbye and people whose bodies had been battered by the furies of war.

Then, Elena Weiss, dignified, stepped down from the cabin and made out the eyes of her son; she made out her granddaughter, Emma, who looked at her with all the delirium and illusion of her thirteen years. She calmly kissed them because she knew she had arrived at a safe haven and she asked for a drink of water, and she handed Joseph a little folded envelope.

Emma Weiss was happy that she had a grandmother who could embrace and see her father and who gave her a present, a golden blouse that had a strange mixture of splendor and poverty, like her family's bonds.

NANA

**A**nd there she was, as if she had been lying in ambush, leaning over my bed, her shawls blazing and she too afire when she buried me in her smell of earth and dry leaves. She came from the deepest, unwary south where the forests make nests of pain. She was eagle-faced, at times a goddess darkened by the years in which she ran barefoot through town with her empanadas fresh from the oven, or with her brothers and sisters, or with their children. And there she was, looking at me, while my mama slept and I felt her breath nuzzling me and at times her hands were a sacred mouth.

She was close-mouthed and stretched out the sound of things. She never told stories but at times when she would mention her land, the green spaces where blind ceremonies were held, her face grew distorted and her lips let off a strange sweat and her body seemed to hang over the edge of darkness.

She came to my mother's house but she never loved it, or her love was a love-sickness, stained and stony, like the agonies of a drawn-out death. She lived twenty years with my mother, she saw her bleeding out through five dead babies, she saw her at night roaming, mutilated, blood traversing the mirrors of the house, and she stood speechless and in silence watching her like a faded bird. As for me, she took care of me, she wove festivity all through my hair. I learned the secrets of cilantro, the longing to make love with the wind, I learned black and white votive candles, I learned to be an invisible presence that sprouted up between the houses.

And when my child arrived she likewise approached his cradle, she repeated winged words, she found out the distant corners and entered them, bit by bit ensnaring him with something that resembled wicked love.

All night long she watched over him as she had watched over me in the house in the mountains. Bit by bit I was giving him to her as an offering that she alone deserved, and I was resignedly losing him, moving further away from his little silky hands, from his lips that repeated only her name.

I was coming to hate and to love her with that strange sensation of those who have their guts pulled out just to have them handed back. I no longer liked her songs sung in other languages or her laughter, demonic, melodical, that scrambled through the rooms. Her presence began filling the soul of the house like a sweaty vapor. She likewise entered my body, making it bleed, and like my mother, I left blood across the mirrors, and at night I hear my body sobbing with the tiny fetus off in a corner like one who hears sea noises at night amid the evil shadows.

Invisible, she lingered around the thresholds. She appeared ominous and beautiful loaded down with lovely things from the market and with herbs, with her face similarly dressed in a thousand masks, and when she bled out the vegetables, I saw that her hands were smeared with the coloring of blood and of fear.

That's how my nana was, she who came to my grandmother's house and then to my mother's, she who came to mine so that I would give her my children and my golden belly, but I strangely loved her as one hears a sound or a voice and obeys it.

Now she's not here anymore, since we had her leave us. She went back to her estuaries drowning in prophecies and curses. She returned to the cavern where mothers join with witches: a witches' sabbath of women alone. I now think of her but my body owes nothing to anyone, it's a box of living children that has learned that gift offerings are touched only by the will of those who give them. Even so, there are times I feel her lying in ambush, gliding over the thresholds, between dead and empty, between mute and aching, taking a seat by my bed as if death were having one last conversation, asking me one last favor, and I smile at her.

MONSERRAT ORDOÑEZ

I never understood why Monserrat Ordoñez had abandoned the winding streets of Barcelona, their shop windows lit by gilt-covered books, and above all the long walks at afternoon's end when the sea seemed to fade into a blue braid of land. Nevertheless Monserrat Ordoñez, unexpected and exact, left Barcelona and crossed inhospitable seas until arriving in Bogotá, where she roamed about as if seeking a resting-place for legends, a place of refuge from the infernal heat that made her go back further to the days of shameless wind. Days when her skirts annoyed her, she'd loosen them while winking at the elegant passers-by who knew that at certain key hours, Monserrat Ordoñez would travel naked along the boulevards. And now, along the Caribbean sea with its slow and strange accent, sheltered under a canopy Monserrat Ordoñez was liable to remain for hours stretched out on the small balcony of her house, which resembled a diminutive bird-cage. The neighbors had lost any idea of her comings and goings. They remembered only sounds in an ancient silence obscured behind the cloud of a crushed Bogotá.

Monserrat Ordoñez desired her solitude above all else, and she spoke of it with love as if for a favorite animal or something stashed away.

No one ever saw inside her bird-cage-like house that was filled with strange perpendicular devices for filtering the Caribbean light. No one ever learned what Monserrat Ordoñez was doing when two votive candles ruled over the ceremony of the onset of afternoon.

One day I spied her in a park near her neighborhood, carrying in a birdcage a mascot, a small ceramic armadillo, that she looked at half-jealously, half-lovingly. I approached her and we spoke of the nostalgia for certain cities that we never quite leave, because of either laziness or strength. She never mentioned the ports of Barcelona or the restlessness of the naked dawns. She repeated to me that above all else she loved her solitude, the paintings of Miró, two or three bourgeois novelists, and monthly attendance at the beauty parlor to leave behind the salt of nostalgia that accumulated in her frenetic, ragged hair.

She said that for twenty years she had lived with no one but the armadillo and a collection of hats donated by the Catalan government.

When I returned to Bogotá, I wanted to meet with Monserrat Ordoñez because I wanted to talk with her of houses and sufferings, but no one knew enough to tell me if she was still staying in the emptiness of her nearby house. Only the woman who watched the door told me that Señorita Monserrat Ordoñez had hung herself because the woman she lived with had left her to get married. By family decree, her ashes were scattered over the Ramblas, in Barcelona, and her face remained hidden behind her hat with its crown of fire.

EMMA

**M**y friend is called Emma, and she's one of those friends for life. For example, we always go off together, the two of us, to the bathroom. Since she was born two days and a month before me, she stands watch for me while I urinate. The word "urinate," like the sound of an old lady's piano, I learned from my friend Emma because she says that her vocabulary and spelling skills are superior to mine. But she always stands watch for me in the bathroom, and she doesn't like it when the others bug us, saying things in our ears, for Emma is very serious. She has black hair and wears blue hair ties and at times I think that her face is perpendicular and she is good; she loans me her hair ties when I have math class, which I absolutely dread.

My momma says that she has no friends for life, that the urgently ladies — that's what she calls them because they are always needing something urgently — they always said "friends for life" but informed on her when she fell in love with a cadet and kept a shocking red pencil by the window of the light meter.

They say that best friends always betray you and so you end up being closest to a mother or to a sister. But I told her that Emma and I are special, that when I think about her she appears to me at times on the corner where we sit down together and share a little bit of fresh bread with whipped butter. We sit very close together and while she is eating she says that she doesn't like the story of Tom

Thumb because nobody keeps track of breadcrumbs. But I like looking at her with her perpendicular hair ties, with her dark eyes like my cat's, and I think that when I grow up, my daughter will be called Emma because it's the name of an empress or a governess.

Emma is my friend for life: I dream of seeing her and telling her things and at times I write letters to her, but I forget to send them and she says to me, "Give me that letter you have in your left pocket." I love her even when she snarls or gets mad at me for eating with my mouth full, but then I tell her those are Tom Thumb's breadcrumbs.

Now Emma has moved to another neighborhood. They arrested her father, but she says that's not true, that her father just crossed the Andes that's all, disguised as a priest. But I know that my Emma's father is in some jail and he really needs the breadcrumbs that Tom Thumb had in order to keep on going and I think that I won't be able to see Emma arriving by the corner whistling somewhere between coy and angry. Also they took Emma's mother off to jail, they said for being a political woman because it's okay to be a woman but not a political one.

Maybe momma is right that there are no friends for life, but I know that Emma can hear me, and that some day she'll get the letters that I have in my pocket because she always told me my dreams, the taste and life's-breath of my words. She is, after all, my friend for life.

WAX CANDLES

For me there was happiness in churches, their wax candles giving sermons, their dim lukewarmth, their delicate twilight silence that rustles when the devout make the sign of the cross facing the figure of that barefoot, sweaty man, deathly cold. I was a little crazed about the smell of incense that spread out into the furthest corners so that it seemed I was entering a perpetual balminess and the air was suspended in the darkness.

Nonetheless, I am Jewish, and I've been aware of it ever since I was a little girl watching my grandmothers Raquel and Sofia, half-sitting, half-squatting in front of the old samovar. They'd sing stories that were like trials and separations, and I knew that I was a traveller arrived from foreign shores, lucky to have survived, to have been able to sense the whiff of other distances, yet I relished the slightest thought of churches and on Sundays at daybreak I'd go off with my Nanny Marisa for all the holy weeks to Sacred Heart where she'd cover up my ancestry, wrapping me in a dense rebozo, and she'd dash me in holy water up to my elbows. Then the two of us would pray, I too saying our father who art in heaven protect me, but I'd ask protection for my grandmother, Sophia, who was eating so much garlic, protection for my sister from the stomach-sickness and headaches provoked by the mediocrity of her husband, and also I'd ask that we be protected from so many earthquakes.

My parents didn't worry about my regular visits to Sunday

Mass, but when I asked them to let me wear a cross of lapis lazuli they began to get anxious. Still, the star of David with all its points did not seem as dramatic and melancholy as the bluish cross. I noticed that they were worried and confused when they asked me stay home on Sundays, saying that I might go with Marisa as far as the front door, that it wasn't so good for people like us to be attending so much church, that they'd call us shitty Jews all the same, reckless trespassers into Christian tradition. But following the defiant tradition of my aunt Eduvijes Weismann who married a Christian and what's more, an uncircumscised one, I kept going with Marisa until one day the priest gave me the host and told me I was eating the body of Christ. Eating the body of this poor crucified gentleman, all chewed up it didn't really suit me, but what really bothered me and left me speechless was to be eating his body in a little cookie and he seemed so incredibly thin with a taste of having been starved. Nevertheless I liked the blue eyes of the young English priest and accepted. And I felt awful for days at having devoured the blood of Christ the Redeemer. After that, I swore off going with Marisa, leaving her instead by the church entrance. While she prayed among the wax candles and illuminated altars, I preferred the patio, the light, the lemon trees.

Now that I'm grown, I love churches and that music which resembles the peace of the dead. Since I'm on a diet I don't eat cookies of any kind, but on sleepless nights I think of how I tasted the body of Christ, and I weep for him.

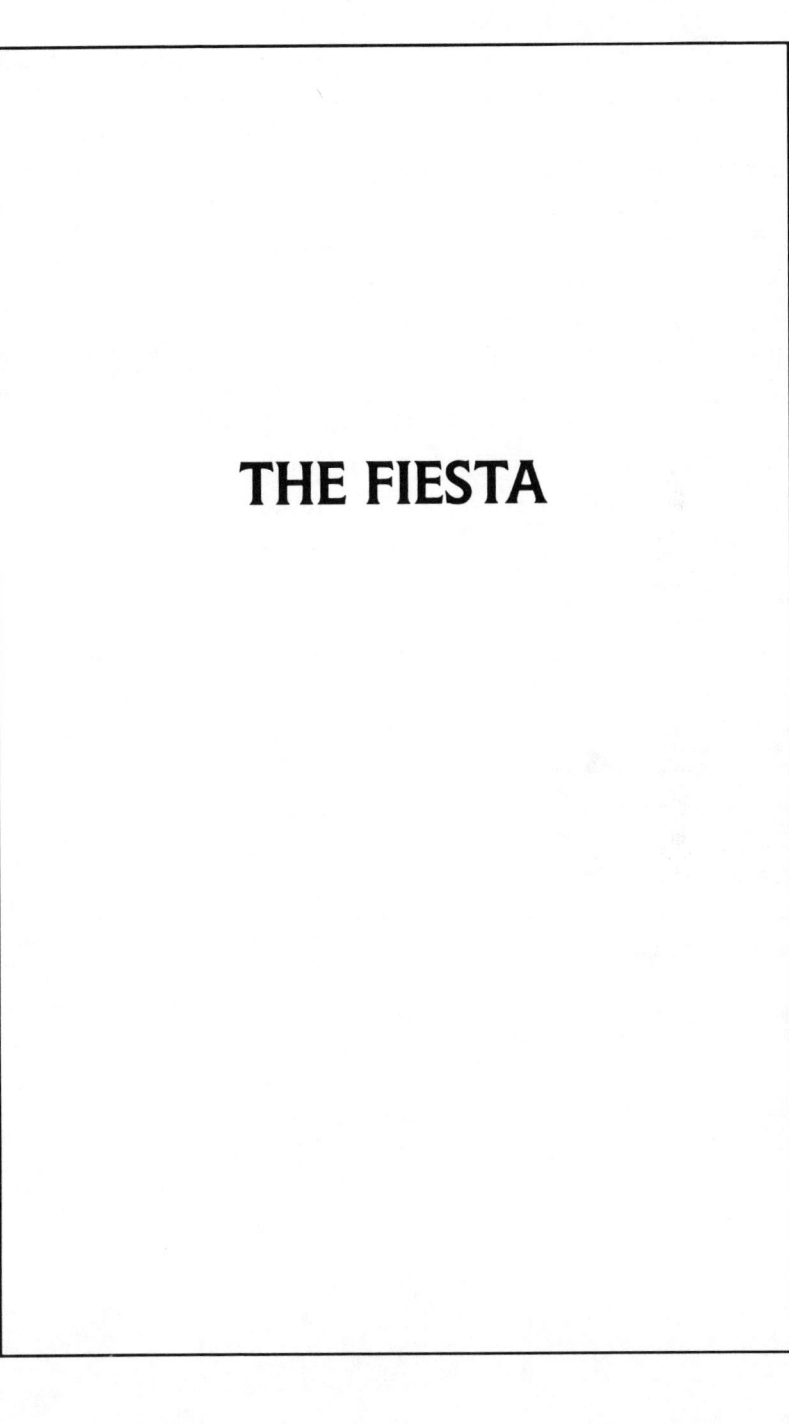

THE FIESTA

GYPSY WOMEN

I always loved Gypsy women. I was wild about them, especially the unruly ones, the irascible ones, the ones who imagined themselves clad in silver threads and jewels even though they were as shoeless and as desolate as their rooms, gnawed at, ferocious. I let myself go in loving their perverse dentures, their insomnias, and their exhausted dreams. I wanted to be one of them, wearing absence under my skirts, feeling with conviction the atavistic pain of knowing nothing beyond the telling of fortunes.

I always loved approaching them, feeling the nostalgia of their gnawing pains, kissing the repugnant orifices of their awkward dentures. Ever since I was little, I would approach those women burdened by rubble and neglect, asking them to read me my fortune or my palms, or the irreversibly, irreplaceably lost. Come closer, they told me, don't be afraid, give me your hand, let me see your fortune, and I would feel that they had dispoiled me of the inferiority of my fancy clothes. I would feel that the percale skirts resembled the dreams of Gypsy women or the longitude of thick, chloroform dreams.

I never feared them, the fortunetellers, because every time that my hand drew near them, every time that my hand was an effervescent rumble of sounds, more than ever I would feel that I desired the irascible calm of Gypsy women, to be one of them, reclining, meditating, begging between good luck beads and evil turns of chance, and it delighted me when they crossed my hand across the paths of my wanderings.

I never feared Gypsy women, and that is why when I approached Gloria Landaeta she was disturbed to learn that I sought neither the stories of the parchment manuscripts that dressed and denuded my hand, nor to learn the mishaps of the immediate future. I resorted to fortunetellers, to Gypsy women, to alms-beggars, to bone-pickers only because I wanted witch #77, Madame Gloria Landaeta, to touch my hand. I did it, and took pleasure in it, so that Gloria Landaeta would caress me and tell me: don't worry, I see a very long life line, I see that some day you will be full of rooms and green-feathered hats. I see death, biting at you, I see a lover in a parachute left nearly featherless in the uttermost ends of the sky.

Gloria Landaeta deciphered the altars of my children, she discovered the precarious nudity of illness. She knew about the transitory deaths of friends betrayed in the maddened anger of abandonment. One time she told me that I, too, would die worm-eaten, like the Gypsies in the backrooms of shops, that I would have a precocious history among the shadows of the underworld, and while I was looking at her, seeking the inventions of my hands, the fortune parlor filled up with the smells of solitude, of two women caressing each other's hands.

Then she crossed my hand with the texture of hers. Dislocated, crazed, she rubbed me with the timidity of an innocent girl, with the indecency of a witch submerged in the very roundness of her story and her muteness. Because when Gloria Landaeta told me my fortune, she didn't reveal disgraces; there was only her hand in that look of hers, that look capable of flooding rivers and forests, like the naked bodies of children being born.

Then, from my hand, those rivers also flowed forth, fish dressed in fog. The movements of love appeared and a line marked pilgrimages as if my hand and hers were a single mirror, and her hand, displacing mine, came to stoneless unwalled cities; it came to the illuminated rooms where the summering of pleasures beckoned.

The years went by and Gloria Landaeta knew my hand, those

shudders that split into stories, those lines more predisposed to love than to perverse solitudes. And although earthquakes, tempests, natural disasters and the penance of the day-to-day were predicted in those unfurled hands, nothing mattered to me, not even the instants when my own death marched along Gloria Landaeta's opaque, transfigured gaze. Because all that I wanted was for this fortuneteller to take me by the hands to preserve the texture, the innocence, the superstition of faith so that this hand would sheathe me like a mysterious throat seeking cover. At times, my hand wanted to hide from Gloria Landaeta, but it couldn't because the two of them had begun to love passionately, and while they grew closer between the beads and the cards, they grew confused and only the prediction appeared, shaped of shells, of secrets, of sounds. Only then, after the terror of the omens of loving, only after the caressing of hands like the feel of the body, I feared magic no more, and preferred above all else the fancy dress of the pain-wracked cards, because I learned that I needed them no more. The magic consisted entirely of her caressing my hand.

NORTH

She arrived in the north without luggage, with the glances of love and the wide green spaces of what now was distant. She wore reddish stockings, and in the palms of her hands bore the trace of crosswinds and fires. They greeted her with the requisite friendliness that foreigners are greeted with. She offered her hand, but they weren't capable of extending theirs because in the north, offering one's hand was a sign of pacts, of intimacies, and no one is able to love immediately, all of a sudden, quickly. They brought her along some noiseless roads where trees and roads mingled with the dance of silence. The countryside was alien to her, meticulously austere, and the snow muted her eyelids.

When she arrived at her room, it seemed to be in a concealed ampitheater where the actors were distanced from themselves in the humiliated circles of silence. They left her quite alone, solitary, and she felt separated, dismembered, as if she were the last guest among ceremonies of bodies pierced through and numb with cold.

They promised that they would return for her after some three days of rest when the citizens of the north neither engaged in dialogue or drank in the marvellous, rhythmical festivals, devoting themselves instead to gathering the embers from their houses and wardrobes, gathering order and pain from feeling alone before love and so close to duty.

She devoted herself to watching the ceremonious snow, ecstatic as a cold sweat amid the fragrances of winter. She stood and looked, wearing her reddish stockings and her soul filling with nostalgia and the trappings of pain and little useful deaths. Then, in the middle of the lawn there appeared three yellow flowers transforming her senses and heightening the relief of the landscape. She remembered the baskets of beans, the chile peppers and the basil and having parsley rubbed on her ears. The flowers made her think of green vegetables, of putting things she loved to her lips, of meeting with lovers in the heart of the plaza. For days she watched them and her entire face seemed to fill up with birds and rushing water, until she decided to gather them up, frigid, blue with cold She gathered them as one who collects in her hands all the softness of the field, and she put them right next to the wounds in her heart. She separated the deadly chill petals. As she melted them she thought of the rivers of her native land.

She was happy alongside the three flowers until the Hostess arrived with that lordly walk and false humility of the powerful. She wore her hair tied back and she wore utterly silent, intergalactic eyeglasses. Also her austerity was monstruously false and distant. The Hostess greeted her with one of those smiles like a knife of false pardon and in her majestic voice asked where those flowers had come from. She told the Hostess how she had seen them appear in the middle of the snow, that perhaps someone had tossed them out and left them in the emptiness. She said that she had collected them, that she cared for them and her hands hovered over them.

Then the Hostess insisted that at midnight she would have to return them since here in the north no one ever stole and the only ones who did steal were people like herself whose coloring wasn't especially light and whose hair snaked about, wild and wavy. The Hostess insisted that she would not let her be until she had returned the flowers to the snow because one doesn't take things that don't belong to one not even the godforsaken leaves of autumn. She said that she would not want to be held responsible for the arrogant irresponsibility of a foreigner and a thief and that even though she had been recommended by people like herself she was doubtful of her being completely honest.

The Hostess dismissed her with that self-certainty typical of the mediocre and the useless, of people who only try giving orders to the humble and to blissfully fortunate immigrants. Then she approached the threshold of a distant ampitheater after she had gathered the three flowers and wove them into her coal-colored hair and at dusk she headed for the field with her heart in her throat as one who goes out to meet up with chance or with some wayward love.

The wind pursues her and she pursues the wind all in a rush of colors, and the blue sky reminds her of the walls of her houses. In her yearning, Mexico charges across her darkened face. Then trembling and sweaty she shapes a hole in the fallen snow where she buries herself, feeling the earth, the pine trees, the green growth that covers and buries her deeper and deeper in the illuminated space of a snowy landscape. The flowers in her hair, the three yellow flowers mingle with her braids and she knows that she is no longer in the north, that she never arrived there. Now she sleeps in the south, south her words and south her voice and the three yellow flowers open.

PHOTOGRAPHS

She would rather unwind along the wind-blown avenues, when the first lights of dawn likewise rested from the tedium of the splintered nights. She strolled with her uncombed mane, her restless steps accustomed to the dangers of evening crosswalks. The city watched over her, preparing strange encounters for her: a lame woman pitilessly beating herself, peopling her body with wounds; some boxes cast aside in the space of the night; and shoeless lovers covered with crusty capes making love among the garbage heaps, howling much like animals accustomed to bringing together the poverty and the pain of those who still love each other between the rough sheets of canvas. Full of scabs, their bodies still know to approach, to obey, to make certain movements that resemble tenderness.

From its reddish-brown case she took a small, battered camera, a box of film for capturing these scenes of love in the backrooms and in the barrios where the rules of the game are violated. On one of her nightly crossings she stopped in front of some old black shoes with strange heels that seemed to have stepped only on riverbed stones. And there were the shoes of some corpse hoping for a wake, waiting to be pronounced profoundly dead in order to be returned to the river, with shoes that seemingly summed up the body of the poor man who wore them Sundays, in pride and in misery.

She carried the photographs as if they were priceless robes

and she hid them away in the remote corners of her garret, taking from them what she nightly portrayed as the gusts of dream and of terror.

She came from a well-to-do family. Her mother kissed her only at bedtime and her grandma filled her with gestures and customs. Grandma, a woman who not only preserved secret brews and riddles but loved her madly, almost with the love of an animal that had been unable to burrow and make itself a nest in the earth. And her mother looked at this strange daughter with her raised eyes and her misshapen hair that lay like the pelt of a watchful, perverse animal, like an unsatisfied, solitary hyena.

When she arrived with the first photographs of two prostitutes showing the eclipses between their legs in a neighborhood circus, her father forbid her to enter the ample mansion. With a grimace of disgust, he forever closed to her the immense, oaken door of that avenue between shadows that had seen her contemplate the broken air through the bars.

But she, delirious, watched over the nights, she ambushed them, and what was horrible to others irradiated her with a pitiless poverty. For her they were exquisite and beloved, and the comings and goings of beggars and of transvestites filled her, more than with pleasure, with light, because she likewise took shelter with them, and she liked it when they touched her at the stroke of dawn as if they were kissing her from within. And when they invited her to drink hot water with a sliver of lemon, it struck her palate, her back, and the cold, too, was pleasant to her.

She never saw her family nor did she witness the baptisms of new cousins. She was nonetheless queen godmother among the tenements, the fairy familiar of the boxers, and the great aunt of the blue-light brothels.

And newly in the night, like a mouth that gasps and pants, she learned of her father's death, but not from the newspapers or television. She learned of it because in the moment of returning from her night-strolling errands, between sleep-walking and drunkenness, there was a man within, green-eyed, wearing an elegant grey suit, who lifted his arms along her legs. Then she knew that Felipe Fuenzalida had died at this same hour thinking of his daughter, taking her waist between his arms, and she could not deny his death. The corpse-odor filled the sheets that assumed the shape of her father's face, with his bent body abandoned to the last instants of sleep. She knew that he had loved her, and she began to shell green peas that seemed like living eyes.

THE GOLD BRACELET

They were one of those couples who on saying goodbye very late at night take one another by the hand with a vague air of separation or of exile. They were one of those couples who tended to make love at daybreak, in silence and disturbed by their solitary public groundskeepers' bodies. Then, rather than further repressing the tones of love and the glances that kept them awake contemplating their own round heaviness, they became all the more tiresome and stingy, hoarding food in the night-stands behind the drapes over secret entranceways.

They never loved one another with desperation or anger. The height of passion occurred when she continued hiding things to eat, imported jams, from the sea-looters. She even had sweet oils and a slice of quince-jelly in the headboard of her bed.

People in the village watched them with concern. She had difficulty sweeping the plaza, gathering the infrequent leaves of an apathetic autumn, and above all, she panted aloud, opening her mouth which seemed like a basket of sausages. He was growing thinner and thinner until he seemed to shrink. Many blamed it on his job in the mortuary because with the plague of '32, with the crash of the economy, the town of Catamarca was burgeoning with strange and perverse deaths.

All that autumn he increasingly resembled a tiny sprig of basil; some swore that he had lost his upper lip and that he was carrying a knotted handkerchief with a vague crimson appearance. Malicious gossips noted that both of his hands were gnawed. Others swore that four and a half of his fingers were missing. He nonetheless continued burying corpses, and the errands of death brought him closer and closer to that region of pain and transparency.

She furtively fattened, amassing gigantic kilos. She seemed to break out in two, and her arms seemed full of immense hands that tore the guts from everything one could possibly devour. They tell about how one day at the height of famine she wound up eating a small sewing machine and her mouth emitted strange sounds like rainbow-colored thread. In the meantime, her scanty husband seemed a shadowy fluttering of wings, especially when the two of them were going home, she loaded down with brooms and he with his undertaker's makeup for repairing the final disfiguring strokes and accidents of death.

By New Year's, or rather, by New Year's Eve, he had already lost any resemblance to a human body and gave the impression of having been dead a couple of days. He seemed to float when he moved, and it was easy to make him out by that strange gold bracelet that hung from his left shoulder. She was utterly delirious. She carried two frozen turkeys and a half-live hen that she ate during her trajectory home while the gold bracelet lit the way for the two of them.

For many months they were no longer seen in town and the corpses came to rest in heaps along the avenues. No one gathered the leaves of a sinister autumn until the town elders decided to enter forcibly the gravedigger's house. There she was, the street-sweep, wide, immense, more immense than the smile of children. Her eyes were glazed over and there was a taste of lunacy, imitating the sway of her feverish hair. A tiny gold bracelet shone on the dining room table.

THE FIESTA

And while she shells peas and arranges fruit in baskets, while she shamelessly begins peeling garlic, Guillermina is a rush of voices that rock back and forth, that tilt as if her body were a single stroke from her shoulders past her foggy, arched waist. Again peeling and quartering fruit as if preparing it for the big night of shouting and love. Because today is the day before the fiesta, Guillermina rises and dresses herself, she slips away. She is a voice full of mirrors while she prepares and dreams the dance of unfurled wings.

It is the dance whose measure of cadences bears ceremonies of goodbye and return. At the entranceway they bring her fruit, mangos, tomatoes, fruit full of leaves for tomorrow's fiesta that will last all week. And it will be seven nights when Guillermina will flower, touching her body as if she were a single fiesta illuminating the branches.

Guillermina begins to work with her neckline, she pulls it down and lays a pea there, in the cleavage. Someone whistles to her and hurries her because more baskets of mangoes are arriving and she sits down with her legs open and the alphabet spinning out from the center, doubled in her memory of skirts that are folded and pleated.

Then, she covers her skin with cilantro because her mother tells her so and says: on fiesta days, cilantro on your earlobes and behind your ears is healthy, it wards off love's wrath. Then she stands up, her step spangled and wearing shoes of her loves' red brocade. They stand out because they glitter, because they may well raise blisters with so much looking and dancing in them. She throws herself into the earth, into the basket of fruit, into her headful of dreams, and her gaze is so glancing because her arms are spread wide with of the colors of the river.

Guillermina prepares herself for the day of fiesta and all the year's savings are for the red shoes and the bluish diadem of endless cut glass, worn across her hair.

And the townfolk see her passing by, down the hill with her shoes that are beginning to twist her before the dance and the sorrow. Her step becomes wetter, more golden, more painful, since there goes Guillermina to the town square so that the travelling salesmen, the kings of magic, the loaned dollars can try their luck with her. There goes Guillermina with her smell of cilantro and hunger. Then she remembers that her mother says don't dance with the first one, hide your neck and obey because the last one is ordained by chance, the children of the future, and the first dance is virginity in between mirrors.

But Guillermina kicks off the shoes in a ceremony of bonfires and pictures. She faints dead away, even to her hair wrapped in cilantro roots, and her body stops exploding. She is a tomb that permits entrance because she wants to be filled with fragrances, because it begins with the rhythm that becomes more difficult, more tense, because sadness is exposed on fiesta days and there is Guillermina, as if she were a daybreak of fruit, a stem of cilantro, a guava in the darkness. They look at her and she dances alone, very alone, happy. She is naked and makes no effort to cover herself; she only uncovers more and more and the red shoe falls very softly and the cilantro tumbles down, and sorrow is a glance. Guillermina dances because today is fiesta day and carefree, and someone kisses her and then she shivers.

ORPHANAGES

In the orphanages I eventually became more used to losing things so that only real-life images — certain forked streets, trees gone to seed in the space of a few hours — held for me the fantasy of distance, a made-up memory of green, growing things and of soothing, balmy encounters. To further preserve the rhythm of what had been lost, throughout the house, and especially in the foundlings' nursery, I hid small, colored stone tablets on which I devoted much time to annotating life.

In other countries far from the sea and the familiar noise of islands, I learned to be happy and to move through the streets as if they were my own. I'd look for the diaphanous edges of sidewalks so that I might make them mine, shaping them to my sleep or insomnia.

More than anything else I longed to return to my country when I died, because I never understood the American way of dying. That's to say, those dead that never in the slightest resembled my little souls when we lit candles for them or when we visited empty houses to speak with them. That's how my dead were. But here they were dressed in red and violet. Days and hours waiting for love-children to travel from California, Nevada, Arizona, a few from the Atacama desert, in order to bury the dead, although doubtless this was just a ceremony for the living.

There were the dead, with their crimson lips, raised chests, and the indisputable coffin odor close by. One dead lady had been perched on gilded wood for some ten days so that she might be buried with her dying daughter. She had been dressed in yellow sheets and her temples perfumed with vanilla extract. Close by, the living commented on the splendid texture of her makeup, the wonderfully brilliant silkiness of her dusting powder, and so did they celebrate her, bringing baskets of fried chicken, carbonated and ordinary beverages. The most adventurous brought one bottle of wine after another, but they did not speak to their dead. It was only among themselves that the living smiled or murmured about the doors of heaven or about the fate of the china and property.

I am desperate about wanting to die in my country where mourning women are not hired, but really exist, where the dead are buried in ceremonies of nebulousness and pain. Where the dead are not painted with makeup because death has its own colored tints. I insist that I be buried in my country not so that they can visit me, or cover me with the jasmines that I love so much, but just to put an end to the ceremony of the living.

THE SEAMSTRESS
FROM ST. PETERSBURG

Because she was Jewish, she could become a seamstress. She kept remnants, brocade, linens under a precarious bed. At sunset just before finalizing her daily missions, such as sweeping under the brass cot, she looked at each one of the remnants as if she desired them, as if they were priceless objects of love, brought from imaginary lands, and she spread them out across the purple quilt. Then she imagined dresses, handkerchiefs, petticoats of beautiful women parading intrepid along the avenues, wearing twine around their heels. Sometimes she spread red lace across her skin in memory of blood and of the front rooms of love.

At dawn she bundled herself in the bulky garments of a scratchy winter and set out in silence for the streets of St. Petersburg, entering by the back doors of the palace where she sewed for the Czarina and her daughters. Little inlaid stones in their thousand shining blouses: meticulously she stopped at every jewel, taking care lest they crash in the park's emptiness. Quietly, doubled over, she embroidered as if she were stealthily praying. Sometimes the Czarina came from very far away to ask who had done this magical embroidery, who had written a fairy tale on her mottled blouse and the seamstress, thin, frightened, fearfully approached. They made her file into the center of the room so that they could see and applaud her, although they all knew that she was an impoverished Jewish woman, young, old, who kept remnants by the foot of her cot.

For years Estefanía embroidered the perfect pearl on the Czarina's blouses and her fingers bore flowers and jewels. A timeless light rocked back and forth with her fingertips because she embroidered with her face veiled and illuminated. Her clothes produced a strange good luck for those who wore them. Returning, dizzy with overcoats, bags full of gilt capes and wind, she made the bells ring and at times the tiredness of her own feet conquered her, drenching her with cold and with what we call sadness.

When they began to kill Jews and trees, to burn hens and Jewish children, Estefanía didn't fear for her weatherbeaten skin or her hunched shoulders, nor did she fear the reprisals of those who foretold the downfall of everyone in the St. Petersburg court. She simply had an immense terror for the valuable scraps of brocade that she kept by that squalid cot of a woman deathly cold amid the disturbing anomaly of that snow-covered city.

One of those days, they burned her room and those on either side of her, yet she kept her most valuable belongings: a thimble of old gold and a very tiny needle brought from the Baltic Sea for sewing the pearls of her distant, beloved Czarina.

No one knew where Estefanía moved to, or how she managed to escape the ceremonies of horror. But they say that they saw her trudging along, tranquil, satisfied, slowly headed toward the outskirts of St. Petersburg, forever leaving that path through the snow, where her sweet footstep through the hostile zones sentenced her to exile. The sadness of her needles embroidered small beads and shrouds.

Estefanía arrived in London. She swept streets, received food through charity and walked with a stoop, aching, as if her body were beating the ground. She was so far from heaven that in order to sleep she joined her tatters and some tapestries with her own basting threads, using the old gold thimble and the needle from the Baltic Sea.

She knew with the certainty of beggars and seers that a relative of the Czarina was parading along in the streets of London, showing that she was still alive. She only wanted to see her and thus to remember those days where they had her sit in the center of the winged room and the other seamstresses looked at her stories made of pearls, her embroidered tales that were like innocent, benevolent sorceries.

And Estefanía scarcely approached her because her weariness grew more intense among the crowds. She listened, in the foreign alleys, to the language of mothers, aunts, of the backroom where the stranger was brought up and embraced like a beloved, wayward pearl from the silent snows of St. Petersburg. The Czarina recognized her. She scarcely bent over to kiss her because she knew she was tied up in the crowd, but she gave her some rubles from her pearl handbag. And thus Estefanía thanked heaven and the spirits, the samovar of her great-grandmother Elena, the first kiss of luck and adolescence and she was able to live in London with the prosperity and abundance of the just. She recovered her brocades and carried them, erect, over her body of silk.

Like so many stories, this is a true story told by my mother, to whom it was told by her mother who came from St. Petersburg and was a niece of Estefanía.

THE EIDERDOWN

for Joseph Halpern

And we prepared quickly for sleep. The mist crackled in the deep heart of the travelling night. We, too, were of a cross-roads, wounded by the pleasure of watching. We were in Austria and I thought of the wounds of my grandfather and of the music of Mozart, like a stream, like a litany, like a fragrance. Then I learned perhaps to be happy in those hospitable, desolate meadows, because the war had erased every trace of scars and only in certain looks were hollow aches and the calamity of dead children still preserved.

Coming onto night, worn through and through by the insinuating byways of hills and greenery, it was in the month of October that Frau Sophia received us. She had blue eyes and her glance recalled bloodless herons. She wore hunting boots and something in her filled me with an implacable sadness, similar to the terror of children in dark rooms.

Her eyes reminded me of the blue sea in the eyes of my grandmother, although she was not my grandmother but rather a strange housekeeper who asked if we would please take off our shoes before entering her immaculate living quarters, and I, terrified, handed her my red shoes. Stripped naked, my feet seemed a backwater of dead fish.

She showed us our room. It had two immense blankets, two eiderdowns whose feathers suddenly assumed the shape and the countenance of blue geese. They were subtle and full of fear. Fatigue and desire deserted us in the country house of Frau Sophia. Luckily, fearfully she assured us that we were her only guests, in the middle of a meadow, in the heart of central Austria, very close to the stone house where they came to look for my grandmother. Because Frau Sophia was seven years old when my grandmother, a beautiful Jewish girl, age eight, was carried off, gagged, toward the plaza of Salzburg.

II.
SILENCED TOWARDS THE PLAZA OF SALZBURG

I take off my clothes but keep the red shoes, ruby red, by my bedside. You lie at my side, defeated and tired, growing old alongside the feather pillows. I know that you do not dream my dreams, but I am happy you are here. Slowly in my gag of fears and without wanting to, you wrap me between your legs as if I were a drunken feathery bird, before love, before births.

I dream of birds, of herons, of the feathers of doves, murderously pale, who carry only messages of war. I dream of noises in the walls and of tied, brutalized hands.

But someone comes to my ear, bringing lilies, singing me a song and filling my skin with love and the bedspread with feathers and knots, with lighthouses and travels. The feathers can no longer shame us because this night, with this return, you and I have called a truce. We have saved life and the name of Jana is cured through the arc of kisses. Are you saying that it's raining or are those love-eyes? You slide over with your legs, you touch, you speak or also sing something about the lilies. All night, someone shakes the feathers, prepares them for winter, blows them, lightens them, almost like springtimes, like birds and trees. My body is a tree with roots of smoke and war.

All night long, like breaks in the night-watch, the bodies are rocking, shaking the down comforters. Then it's time to wake and again that someone is shaking the huge down comforters, or it's your calm, careful breathing tied to my own throat of feathers that likewise dreams.

III.

dreams after war
skin covered with love
women with happiness
in their bellies, and the calm of feathers
rests
in our body.

PISAGUA

I entered the grave site at Pisagua one ancient evening when it was very dark despite a tenuous moon that shed precocious beams. From far away I made out the tiny lights of the harbor and the strange, occasionally perverse odor of smoke that also drifted into the grave.

In the distance the sea seemed to have recovered the shadows and the sound of distances. At times I imagined meeting myself in the silhouette of those corpses. That night when I went almost on my knees into the grave there was no meeting anything, not even the noise of seagulls circling over the excavated bones.

A strange and almost absent voice told me to search no further, that all of them had already been carried away, the five disinterred bodies. The darkness kept me from making out that man's face, but his voice reminded me of worn wood and upturned earth.

Brusquely, I wanted to behold his silouhette straight on, to feel it, to ask him how had he arrived without my seeing him. I wanted to ask if he knew when they had been carried off. Was it possible to recognize any of them?

I was disappointed on understanding that he might well be a guard, above all when we were immobile in the center of the grave. Then when I saw him with a shovel digging in circles around a tunnel, then I said to him:

"You're not a guard."

"That's right," he responded, "I've been coming here twelve

years now, looking for my son."

Then I too began with the shovel to look for his son who was mine and in the same emptiness of the night we repeated the ceremonies of the shovels. We excavated immense graves and when we drew close to one another to contemplate our faces, we howled like dogs in the night, in Pisagua, when the dead finally managed to bury the living.

SIGNS OF LOVE

THE HEN

All night, all through the dismal, lonely night she dreams of buying the hen because that's what her sons and her son's wives have said and her husband has repeated it, that she must bring a medium-sized hen, neither too plump nor too dry, a recently-slaughtered hen, with wings like the rhythm of velvet. Because tomorrow she will celebrate the seasons, the fertile times, it is absolutely necessary to have this hen and what's more, even its blood should gush like that of live hens. All night she begins thinking about buying the hen as well as the cilantro, the lemons, the shells covered with water, the herbs, and she is frightened knowing that she must prepare the immense list of groceries, knowing that neither gods nor men will protect her if she doesn't arrive home with the perfect hen, and they are still saying that she must take care that the skin be very tender, like the craters of sleeping volcanos, for otherwise they will have bad luck in the harvests and the land will fill up with menstrual blood, the lakes will turn bitter and the fish will die and she, all through the night seems a blanket full of expectations, her hair twirling like the deadly melodies of what dies and becomes nightmare. Then she seeks some cure for sleeplessness, and they have told her to cover her sheets with tulips as red as the blood of the hen that she must bring, like the blood of that hen that will be recently beheaded and she only knows that she must wait for the first noises of dawn, she must wait barefooted for the aching daybreak because they need a freshly-killed hen to come to the house and she also knows that before looking for the hen she must have the fire lit, the empanadas prepared, the water rolling at a boil, stammering the onset of day and also she should write a poem and let the dogs out and the birds in from the cold because they are all calling her and she in the dark room lets herself be carried away by their voices and in the silence, she notes that she must bring the transformed hen that must have skin as fine as laminate and be chubby like the sky on holidays and everything tells her that the hen, the chicken, the birds are what's most important in eternal life above all when recently the soul seems half dead and she feels so transparent, so close to the water, knowing that she must look for a hen so that they don't cut her throat . . . yet.

PORK SAUSAGES

He never was greedy, but I knew about his satanic and benevolent perversity when, in the rounded edges of late afternoon, he went crazy slicing little bits of pork sausage that he would eat with the delicious compulsion of perverse wolves and saints. I never feared his odd ways or his disfigured neck that reminded me of the dry hens in the neighborhood, and I delighted in being merely the new teenaged girl, the rotten desire of his desires, when he closed me up in the dark rooms, the unreal backrooms where we summered. Dry-eyed, we believed in magic, like hyenas dressed in hunger, like sea shells, like summer.

We spent long seasons in the crystal room where we sneakily watched over the visit of some strange summer visitor, especially little blonde girls whose hair was like straw from the brooms that inhabited the outskirts of his house. He wanted to make himself loved so he could betray them later. At times, he managed to like them, but only rarely would he let them lay alongside him through the long and sinister night.

On the other hand, I was permitted, or, better said, he permitted me to remain in his narrow bed that was like the backbones of dead whales, his bed where he contemplated the concave mirrors of our precarious nakedness. I delighted in being there, so near and so naked. His body seemed the sad souls of sleep. He no longer had wrinkles and a loose neck; he was no longer decrepit. He straightened himself up like a proud and magnetic canvas. He had the habit of making tattoos on my shoulder and he liked to see me laugh at every word. We loved each other for many years. We were strange next to the rocks, or on the winter beaches where we ran precariously across the sands, collecting and plucking feathers from dead gulls. Yet this strange and strict happiness came to an end when Menchu approached our house. With wooden candles she poked at us, choleric, enraged, jealous of my face with yours, with our love like that of crazy children.

All night long she spied on us through the crystals, and her face was that of a hyena in dense smoke. All night the sea and its fog banks and her irascible footsteps against the pock-marked wood until it was impossible to strip ourselves naked because all those faces of Menchu and her tribe of sisters intervened, and I could not make your loose hair a tangled forest across my face.

We wanted to frighten her, but the brooms that had been our only weapons shamelessly lost their tresses. At night when Menchu and her twin sisters raked through our manes, hair sprouted up from the ground, coming up to the sky of the windows. She made it sprout, and we finally managed to lose them in the sinister landscapes of my hair. Little by little we were alone. Solitary, we'd pass hours and hours braiding and unbraiding, although you had the crazy and sane habit of looking behind you, as if someone wanted to slit your neck. That's why you chose round tables, so that only I would be able to tattoo your hair.

Throughout the years, no one intervened in our landscapes, and my body grew as your neck did but without the encircling wrinkles. I had children by others, but only in your mouth, only in your short fingernails did I meet a carpet, a challenge of yellow leaves and blankets of affection. Your smile watched over me in sweet company for years, those years when I invented you, younger and younger, resting along the edge of the rooms, without stage-settings or representations, eating pork sausages and with no tribe of Menchus piercing our nakedness.

ITINERANTS

For Susana Cárdenas

There they were, crouched and hidden between the doorways and the wandering trails of the lights. They smelled of restless cold and even the smallest ones didn't dare wake early on a furious morning, restless and thin with cold.

Moribund, frozen, they seemed to have emerged from the famished onset of night as they went into the journey toward dawn. They embraced each other in those lightning-quick caresses that knived across their backs: these were their acts of love, when their movements would fearlessly flower, for fear was still unknown, although they numbly hurried to tidy their cardboard boxes, to improvise the small shops of a terrified, precarious world. Then they piled provisional altars with cheap plastic, gilt bracelets and they raised their hands, the hands of hungry women from the countryside. Then they let go of those boxes of plastic and battered cardboard that resembled the traces of a tight-rope.

And they began
to shout, they violated us shouting
they tore out guts
they tattooed the sidewalks
they were blindfolded
and the placid faces of those who set out at daybreak
were detained.

They asked how much did the plastic brooms cost, what color was the yoyo, before, asked the ties and the placid faces as they approached the plastic set-ups, appalled and smiling.

And again, someone fluttering, emitting groans: then it was known they were warlocks, that the sidewalks, the cities and the bridges were filling up with warlocks, and that it was the warlocks who prescribed poison weeds for good luck. It was the warlocks who tugged at the hands of passers-by, to help them slip off their rings, to empty them out, empty, and thus to draw out their luck, despoiled, brave, in a second or third nakedness.

And the cities of idleness, of live prostitutes, filled up with magicians. Grass sprouted in the voices of people whose teeth had been knocked out, for there was good luck in knowing how to stare, to feel the wave of terror in their breathing, and to accept the warlocks as if they too were love's bystanders who looked at the opposite end of the sky

> for they are incautious and distant
> for they are the warlocks
> who see the future in the beginning
> of the frost on the trail
> of the empty fingers.

WATER

So you're going to throw yourself into the river, you haven't stopped looking at it, fascinated by the abysmal paleness of the waves? Haven't you stopped tossing poisoned pebbles so that at times you resemble a dancer while you look at it as if, with your eyes, you were learning to fill yourself up with water? What do you dream with your starched, fishlike stare? That you like being just so you can pass interminable hours in the scenes of the rivers?

It has been two years since your death and only two days since they found you in the Hudson or in the Aconcagua, devoured by the river fish that you loved so much.

Are you going to throw yourself into the river because you want a crown of water flowers, a burial of sands, because you want to fill the sea city with dead fish? There you are. I surprise you again at the edge of the precipice at evening's high tide, hoping that someone helps you in, navigating for the last resort. Then, I am the woman who approaches to restrain you, drawing your waist near mine and making a river.

So I cannot go crazy now. I was only a sensible, maimed woman announcing your death. It rolls me up, strangles, revives and collapses me. Are you gone again to the river, not just because you want to, but because you want to travel, to roam, to feel yourself remote, lost near the bottom of the blue well? Then I betray you, I shout, explode into noise amid the tides, telling them that you are about to throw yourself into the river, your head about to become a sunflower of strangled fish, that in these very moments you are setting out for the river and they are calling you, restraining your waist that is also mine.

They may tell me that I have been going crazy, that I am one more lunatic woman among the plateaus, that I am newly born among the abysses. They tell me that you have only gone for a walk along the river and perhaps you disappeared for a couple of days in order to feel absence. But I shout, howl, beg that it is true, that you have thrown yourself into the river, that I have seen you erratic, tranquil. Then I knew with that untamable certainty that you went off to the parks, to other cities or maybe another country. But I look at you and I see you in the bottom of the water, in the bottom of my empty body, in a watery graves without flowers.

At night, you approach my skin as if I were the very depth of the water, like funeral biers, like the caresses of cornered deaths. And at times our words have the sound of rivers, the longitude of desolate coasts where our bodies seem lost altars of mangled seaweed.

SIGNS OF LOVE

His body in the nakedness of the winged room left spaces. At times he resembled a history of roots inclined between the shadows, and the light was a wheel of mirrors and of nooses. His body resembled a starry quietude, it was dark and smelled of the forests, of damp rainy wax.

At times I see him, I feel him reclining on a sea of blue clouds and the way that he draws up his legs or tightens his lips makes me think of happiness. Then we draw close to one another. I believed in love and it seemed to me that from the alcove some watery liquid was flowing out, like what lies within water and watches us from the bottom.

Often, debilitated and aching, we'd stay in the silence of the vulnerable, of people in love. Restless, full of lusts, but with humility, he shaped houses, braids, stories born from the fringe of my hair and coming to him like bewitched fish. When he wrapped me in his skin, when we'd repeat the glances of love, he was the summary of all those who had loved, and again that atmosphere like darkness and light and once again his eyes like two dark rooms where I initiated myself in perversity and the parties that circle over reclining bodies.

Then, accustomed to the rites and the tattoos of the skin, he would go off at the break of day, mixing rancor and hatred, and his body would remain, caught, slow, even agonizing in my moribund glance that required him to lie down in order to return to thinking of love.

Each night it was useless to weave his dreams with mine. For that reason he avoided sleeping face down, and he touched my hair making small chains with it. Then each night he would go off leaving a singular shape in the very center of the bed. One time it was a flower that danced transfigured along the cracks in the semi-darkness. The flower was a butterfly of sleeping mouths rocking in the tranquil waves of the sheets. One night, disturbed by the rains, his body left the outline of pine trees. It seemed that the smell of the border of sleep left indecipherable emblems of solitude and sadness on the sheets of love.

At times I longed for his habitual but disconcerting trek in order to see the threads of his somnabulent body stretched out, shining, and to travel along the blue sea canvasses that were our sheets. One night I thought that he had left me his eyes, and the alcove was increasingly dispirited, bereft of shadows and only his eyes made more hollows in my body. Often I longed for him only to await his escape, his abandonment. I would people myself with the real images that emerged from the incessant nights of love, and to see after his distance the strange and gorgeous forms that his body was leaving near my anniversary: he left a dove's countenance, and some green feathers scattered along the space that his lonely, sad legs had occupied.

For years we caressed one another, or perhaps it was only two months, boat trips through strange cities, through the imaginary cathedrals of love, and we would repeat that no one could ever love as we did, thrown together into bed like the absent, like the dead, buried in worlds that do not speak. We would caress each other like what is made and is remade in dreams.

It was on that anniversary when he decided to leave before the break of dawn. My hair was ensnared in the ceremonies of goodbye and the darkness of the room filled with the soul of the fireflies, though we knew that only a silence of gnawing rodents accompanied us.

Once he was gone, images no longer remained on the sheets and an absurd fear began to grip me as if I were suddenly losing everything, even the body's perpetual pleasure and the nakedness of the debris left behind in every night of love. Then I suddenly saw that his hands were two closed stumps and his legs a starry, bladeless knife, just like everything that is dark, that dies of cold, that has no shadow.

LOVE LETTERS

His letters began to arrive marked by the innocence of words that resembled sounds. They became greetings that sometimes spoke of the morning as being a turquoise sky. Once he sent a feather from a female bird and wayward drops of perfume scattered from the body moments before love.

She awaited his messages submerged in the desperate clarity of patient women who begin to come out of themselves, who tremble when someone calls them with a loving voice, and the handwriting recalled summer caresses that begin fully dressed and end up with wrinkled stockings singed with smoke and that exquisite shame of the little delirious crimes of love but she, alone, rose with the dawn to hear along by evening the quick steps of the mailman, and she would wait for that desolate hour of late afternoon so that she might sit by the water repeating the words again and again, even entering an abyss, rubbing the paper against her body, against her eyes.

She longed to see him cross over the great spaces of the garden, to feel his entire body long before his words, to imagine the taciturn presence of his hands that were like forests of smoke burying themselves in her body.

The letters remained safe, and she kept them in the trunk of caresses until he asked for a meeting in the railyards where the trains stood empty, at the corner pastry shops and she laid awake all night long, captive to sweat and to fear. Seeing him would be feeling his mouth like a word, seeing him would be losing her mind and the peace of waiting daily, that leaf that forced her into flower like luminous daylight and inclement weather.

She chose silence as if it were a spiteful lover. She chose the solitude of her legs, bound and gagged. She chose the wearied rereading of those love letters, losing breath and life to protect them yet never seeing that censor who, close by her house in a false and wholly imaginary distance, was writing them to her in the inclemency of his body, lulling himself to sleep between bedclothes and the chill air.

FIRST TIME TO THE SEA

Quite close together, in the warmness of shared bodies, they dared to dream of the sea. Some imagined it as the deep well of the soul; others sketched it out like the face of a drowned man, weighed down with broken seaweed and shells. Every night they tried to speak of the sea, and the older ones consoled the youngsters that they had to wait some years yet, for their turn to make the longed-for journey to the coasts, to the blue frontier of water.

At times they pulled from feather-dusters bits of orphaned plumage and they'd pretend to be roguish and disoriented seagulls. And then they sketched sea-spells on the other side of the sheets. Among the semi-darkness of threadbare poverty, they'd recount the spells of night, because their naked bodies resembled cities that still lacked shores, glittering lights, ground-swells.

Someone raised them: hurried, they drank a foreign milk while the cutting edge of the floor tiles woke them early. They were so full of absences that all illusion betrayed to them a solitude far beyond their poor little bodies that were as bent and as curved as the arc of night. Then, after the crossroads, they saw it in the distance. There it was, splendid, like an immense blue landscape. There it was, seated and wide, and the eyes of the children filled with its colored ashes. And there was the sea, casting spells with its innocence and its inhospitable ill-will, full of the most merciless, most handsome of drowned men, the most sorrowing widows, but it was the sea, the brave sea of the coasts, the sea full of broken seaweed and crazed fish.

They drew near, fearful, sleepy. The most innocent among them offered his cracked, shabby foot. A starfish caressed it, and the sea was implacable, terrifying, staring down the watchful gaze of children who dreamed of renting swimsuits. Panting, terrified, they looked into its grey depths to discover the treasures of the night. And there was the sea, drifting and full, peopling the sand, the buried children, children anxious for the latest swimsuits. They longed to submerge themselves in it, to be able to outline themselves in its caresses, poor children who had never looked at the sea, who sought only to rent used swimsuits, to shape their conquered little bodies in the indifferent longitude of the waves.

MIRRORS

She set to collecting mirrors, concave ones, round ones, or those that with time and repeated moves from one house to another had lost their acuteness. But she stored them under wraps. In the wounded darkness of the night she set them next to the very darkness of desire. Every night, naked, transparent, molded from a timorousness like the outlines of death, she looked at herself, especially in those splintered double mirrors, those symmetries that time had left until leaving her empty, bereft of birds.

Occasionally, she chose cracked mirrors, hoping for prophecies of unlucky times because in them she could see the middle of things or the middle of life surrounding the hole of broken glass.

Then she travelled languid and possessed by rivers, but especially in feverish deserts and in the luminous prairies that mingled with the noise of passing water. She contemplated herself as if she were a gigantic mask tattooed with amnesia.

The navigators, those who are liable to be friends with the desert and the night, say that they found her formally dressed and full of silence, her body sliced through by anger, with slivers of glass adorning her face between the shadows.

MEDITATION ON THE DEAD

In autumn when light filters through the sweet and crackly air, in autumn when the slivers of leaves seem goblets of yellow wine, she devoted herself to visiting cemeteries. Between the leaves, she joined the names of the dead to return and shelter them with yellow's density because the dead like it. She listened to them arriving at their tombs between the whisper of pines. At times she had a foreboding of them. Then she entered the hospices as one who enters with her whole heart into the rhythm of a poem. She liked to approach them, to tenderly match their brows, to meet them at the sound of the last flutter of eyelashes over their faces, to bathe and dress them in the open, intrepid night.

Morning and night she would speak with her dead, preparing invisible suppers for them and speaking with them of the ceremonies of death and of love. All night she held the secret ceremonies of those who keep watch over the dead, but she delighted in this labor, which was so submerged in the very sphere of the earth.

This autumn with its yellow airborne ribbons reminds her of walking along sidewalks towards cities, directionlessly, towards those who are buried in the most concave and remote of silences. Then I spy her by the roadside, weaving words with mint. I don't stop to ask her whose turn it is now, but I see her as if buried in inconclusive glances of water and predictions of fallow times.

The townspeople follow her. They say that she prepares banquets, that she lights her twilights with torches made from crippled bones, and that at her round table she places cadavers collected from childhood, but the seats are always empty, the razors, the doubled braids of time. All in its place as if she were awaiting an opportune moment because she too wants to die, she wants to be a pillow of autumn underneath her shadow, she wants trees to protect her and fondle her in the foundations of winter. There she is waiting to die because she can't die. She calls out to them between the crystals and she, dauntless, grey, awaits the day when someone will carry her off, preparing for her, too, an invisible supper, some white walls, a silence-filled cave and a last supper's bread.

RIO DE LA PLATA

As those who search for happiness or its glitter, their voyage was launched in a boat that hung from the movement of sea and land alike. She wore her hair loose and panting, over her shoulders. It twisted round her body amid the constant booming of the sea. They were travelling, lost and nocturnal, keeping a watchful glance on the shapeless distance. He did not want to speak about things of war, about the times that they had ordered his hands to bury living eyes.

She only begged him that the things from the sea might speak or moan in that silence that was more terrifying than the night, for the angels of war had marked their heads with the spectres of the decapitated and the fingernails of the disappeared swarmed through the cabins.

The ever-present tourists drew up to the bar, holding their liquor poorly. One tango melody after another accentuated perverse reminiscences. She remembered when from the very depths of her bed she feverishly went off as if bewitched, searching for other bodies to repeat the rites of fear, to stuff herself with happiness through the sufferings of others and thus choose to approach death up close.

The far-away music with its air of abandon made her cry at not being able to take refuge with him, perhaps an innocent jailer-captain of crimson mirrors, as they told him in the maddened nights.

They grow evasive and distant. The night shadows that emptied out begin entering in a summer-like mist. Her hair stands on end, strangling the landscape of the topmasts. It cautiously aims for the rooms occupied by the government authorities, the rich families still fighting over inheritances from the dead.

They strip naked, innundated by sea-shadows, anchored to the ancient customs of human navigations. And as the river blinds their faces, they can no longer be startled in the darkness of the sands. The river disfigures them. In vain they try to find clarity, but something submerges them, the Río de la Plata: it is so thick, so ashen. From the very bottom of the riverbed there explodes a human storm of things, of hands, of eyes, of those very hands that years before had split the booty of the police. She sees them shine, the loose fingers along her wavy hair. Someone hears a howling across the pillows swaddled with the names and the clear zones of the body. They began to fill themselves up with corpses. Then he told them about the wars along the tributaries of the Río de la Plata, about the missions from the helicopters.

Her hair innundates a crazed face. It was even stranger than when they had set off in search of a happiness of aching bodies, because here were the dead, in the very bottom of the river, their bodies filtering the sunlight, drying out the wounds in the sun, leaving life to the sun. Restoring life to the sun.

FORESTS

BLOOD

How to talk about Blood, how to say it, to make it, to see it, like a sloping Aztec thread resting across the split of the knees, making a knot of scarlet crowns unstitching the orchard that covers our feet. How to speak to you, Blood, who bring me close to life and bring the pieces of death back to me. Annihilated, incredulous, I try to detain you with a look. I try to rescue you from the chill of that indifferent but never foreign body that receives you. Then you seem like the rivers of the wakes, then you seem like the fragility of the kisses, of those dull but loving summers, then I bend over to pick you up. But this time you stop me, as if it were my hand or a trunk sprouting from the very articulation of language.

Blood, how to tell you don't come close yet, don't arrive yet to bring me dead children. But you pierce through me, you wrap around me, in the nets, in the forebodings of night. Then in the stupor and darkness I contemplate you. You seem the color of the desert, of watermelons, you seem a flower in front of rocks in the sun, and in your amorphous goodness you let me see scraps of life, fresh strips of meat, a dead child gravitating between my legs and my memory. Blood, how to tell you?

You start out like an omen, like wayward, wrinkled drops of honey from trees. You appear like a portent of evil. I look you over as if I were handling some long-vanished, precious stones, but you are only a small, infinite sliver of dead, smoky flesh. You begin working yourself into the very roundness of my body. Descending, you calmly cross, not wanting to be untimely, but your arrival is familiar to me. I indecisively wait for you to set yourself loose, for a season of rains and rivers to embrace my legs, turning me into an immense hand of live, dead blood. So you shift about as if you were a madwoman, raving drunk. I too look at you as if none of this were happening to us, as if we were some sinister characters from a second-rate opera.

Unhealthy, you approach me. I look at, study you, seeing that you are beautiful, very red, like watermelons, like the color of desire, but like the death of what cannot be at that insignificant onset of human life.

We are together, hoping that in a dizzying split second you will give up, that what remains of what had become life would be unmade, that it would leave, angry and dead, from within my legs, not burying it, not even blessing its coagulated shadows, so that I may rest at last, my body once more becoming lanky, independent, closed.

I want an end to this funeral of the living. I ask that you let me be, that you don't come near, that you don't make me bleed more. Yet you continue, wild and intrepid, resembling new-born frogs that push off and are vanquished, wheeling across the bitter soil.

I rest in peace, I begin to live, I begin to die, lonely and languid. Defying destiny, I yell. I don't say I'm sorry. I yell.

JOURNEY TO THE END OF THE COASTS

I approach coasts as if I were an imprecise navigator or a far-away vagabond circling over the sands, seeking out fire, beginning to know myself and to deliver the light from the very bottom of my eyes, eyes that blink when they look toward what is fused from the very skin and breaks out in the waters'-edge of my coastal regions.

I wander along paths and seal rookeries until arriving at a wooden house with the names of the dead carved on its shutters, a house that smells of suffering and flames. No one awaits me. I return as a bride widowed by love.

From far away I listen to the sing-song moaning of drunks and of superstitious children who carry houses in their hair, and of some wounded man who, after spending nights at sea, returns but never to the drifting sands.

I strip naked and approach the gusting wind, and I repeat the night rituals. Turning on lights, I open windows out of timidity and fear of these rooms facing the sea and of the bodies of the drowned whose parade makes of my vision a glance of blood. I am returning, approaching the sea that frames the soul, the body of the island that breaks off from the land to form a solitary death that searches for the ribs of buried ships.

A strange orthography begins peopling my body with sounds; the scent of lime-encrusted winds anchors in the very heart of the night and someone begins stitching up my mouth so that it will be a kiss stolen in the silence of the sea.

Someone is approaching; it is a handsome drowned man and his mouth has the ceremonious shape of coasts; I am solitary and happy. I draw increasingly near the window that gives him shelter and light. The night is a lake of phosphorescent water, the drowned man, fierce, triumphant in his legendary dampness. He picks me up, he covers me with water that is violent, white with foam—I am a rhapsody of all the dead, I am an archipelago, a coral reef, a lighthouse of melodies and the drowned man kisses me, celebrating the wedding of the seas, he kisses me and with wet chalk outlines my name in the whirlpools of water, he slips me away, he brings me to land, he bears me as if to the bottom of the sea. They told me that they found me mouth down, naked as a solitary bride in the embers of the corals, at the end of the coasts.

FORESTS

Furtive and timid, she readied herself, waiting for love, lighting candles in the cabin, her very body blazing as bonfire in the captive days of autumn. She was waiting with the desperation of desire, angry and violent, for a night of love in the cabins, in the forests' depths. She was waiting naked, unwary, solitary; she imagined him arriving among the swamps and amid the noise of the leaves beneath his soles, above his hair. She, too, smelled of mottled autumn, tepid and gloomy. Then he arrived and his steps made her tremble, confusing her body with the gloomy vastness of the forests, and they stripped naked in the immense mirrors of pitiless trees.

They kissed each other with the laughter of the violent seasons; they copiously repeated things in one another's ears. She defended her body but promised him chances and secrets all the same. Then when the night had made a dangerous well between their bodies, he prepared to go back, stepping over her like leaves in a ferocious dusk. She begged him to make of her hand a plateau over the sea but he only gathered dry leaves to bury her in a silence of bald women, to imprison her in a treacherous, intermediate season, and she, moaning, naked, wildly in silence, she sweetly asked him for a little bit of shadow to ground her in the treetops, to be clothing in his hands.

He went away caressing her as if through habit. Only the sound of his intense, throbbing footsteps, the very opposite of meadows and trees went with her in the seasons of autumn's melancholy dark, its shadowless days and nights. Lost, she slept face down like a traitorous root in the body of a solitary woman.

BEDS

I.

beds like an ocean, like seaweed strands, hair where every-
thing swirls and takes shape, anointed by threads and fine string,
beds like love all night long and the drunken body displaced and rul-
ing over the mazes of desire which is sleep, face up, face down

II.

beds for making of the body the exact text for knowing
where the caress is buried, where lips shelter what has been said,
beds so that the living may imagine death and dream of it as a cere-
monious angel lying along the water's edge in the onset of door-
ways, beds like coffins that divide us and make us fall into another
world where we may arrive late yet all in one piece

III.

beds where women stretch out and kick off their shoes, open-
ing up and shrinking as if the body were but one wound: wild and
tender, they give birth, beds are also blood fanning out, a wide,
tumultuous avenue of lives and rivers, of the tiny bones of the
newest born, the drenched deathbed: a halo of flesh.

IV.

beds for sharing betrayals, for turning love into orgies, with the body's secrets playing at war's fury, at the miseries of brave generals who leaning back in bed think of other beds, of torturing and the complicitious bed prophesies their tremendous deaths

the bed where I begin to dream of the lights of the air where I melodiously strip naked and engage in my body's chores

then I approach it, wide and spread out as a fresh flower, smelling of words and of songs, smelling of my mother in days as nights

waiting for me, receiving me, it is noble in its blonde timbers, generously sheltering me, I dream of death and the accidents of life

the bed where you and I did not meet in the days as nights in the nights as days, beds where the gestures of all men are repeated and we become a single mirror, the wound of all women and I am a light, weighed down with shadow

in bed we love one another belonging to one another we understand the world lying flat on our backs horizontal vague noble

CARTOGRAPHIES

Letters read aloud, asking you to read and re-read them to me, again and again, as if you were brushing my hair, as if you were beginning to strip me naked until filling yourself with my body that crosses through you while approaching you in a single nakedness.

Love letters or Dear John letters, angry words so that you read them to me as if your voice were a secret in the very secret of a rounded word, and disturbed by your voice that rises, that picks up like the very glance, stolen, that is inlaid in my ears. Because love letters that aren't read fade away.

And she reads love letters in the immensity of the air, imagining that her voice has the resonance of stone and of rivers, she imagines dreaming about what is said and is said to her in these letters, and at times she calls herself to hear herself in the shout and suffering of words, and to make of the letter a body, a face.

Letters stashed away, laid by in the placidity of memory or dreams that rescue them, and she makes her forehead perspire with certain words, and she reads them, she looks and she makes them and unmakes them because it seems that they are as right as rain.

The moaning that lies behind the syllables; and at times although gone crazy she seems to listen to the knife's-edge of laughter, and she drinks down the syllables as if it were life itself that had reached her, that snatches at her with the precision of a wise witch.

In letters he confesses: he never saw the flowers that she left on the breakfast table, he never saw the bird's egg that she wrapped in paper for him, and he tells her that he buried bundles of hair on the island that faces the sea, and also he tells her that his skin is already an absence that became a tattoo in her word. She reads.

Love letters, to be read aloud so that they don't fade away, so that they become a braid in my hands, an immediate, winged certainty: love letters so that they don't fade away must be read aloud.

THE DEAD

I.

We had the custom of visiting cemeteries, of examining tree trunks, the base of the earth's density. We were hoping to speak with the dead, to roam among the newly-born tombs, to give them a greening leaf, curly with sweat.

II.

We never had to leave the cemetery by the entrance road. What's more, ceremoniously, we would wash our hands, wringing, scrubbing them roughly so that death would not enter along our watery arms.

III.

She spoke with her dead children. The one who fell from the sky in a traitorous parachute was called Marcos, the son, but we all called him little Marcos and another little Marcos had been born, to bless him. She spoke with her dead son, asking him to teach her to cry. In his tomb there grew little flowers, pink like the face of his mother who kissed him in the days of his life.

IV.

Everyone tells me to visit him, that he is in vault number two alongside the two youngest gentlemen whose sad fate made them leave Earth. But I insist that he isn't in the cemetery, that his soul still hasn't arrived, that I saw him near Wall Street and just a few hours ago, winking at a beautiful, enigmatic woman selling Brazillian coffee. I know it's true that he died in the murky waters of Lake Vichuquen but I nonetheless saw him in the street. He embraced me thus very sweetly and we said good-bye, calmly this time.

V.

When I think of how his son is dead, his living father's face fills with plagues and absences. When I look at him I know that he will never be able to dance the Russian dances of blood. Then I know that his mourning is perpetual, that his son's death has cut from him the sounds of the heart, the speech of dance, but he does not move.

VI.

I sleep with my dead. They approach the roundness of my bed and visit me often. On dangerous days, Aunt Olga arrives with a sharpened broom to scare away evil spirits. On temperate days, my grandfather, José, returns to the forests with his summer-green eyes. Then I know that it is the fertile season for planting lilacs.

VII.

The day before yesterday my great-grandmother Sonia arrived, the one from Odessa, the one who went to sea barefoot with eight small children in a dark warboat and came all the way to the shores of Chile to buy eight pairs of shoes. She told me of the arrival of a tiny little Sonia with violet eyes the color of Odessa seagrass. She repeated strange blessings, but I could hear only her kiss in my belly.

THE RUBBER TREE

To José María

It all started when they brought this little rubber tree that resembled children who have been dwarfed and unable to grow for want of the never harsh strokes and caresses that they need. So they brought it. It seemed swaddled, terrified, kept in a strange clay planter. They set it at the edge of a little park that with its imposing trees could still shelter small children who dared steal out into the darkness to pet the hunger-bedraggled dogs who roamed the cities.

There was the rubber tree, so dignified and humble in the middle of the empty plaza with its ruined paper lanterns and one retiree after another seeking the embers of heat at daybreak.

That's how the years passed in the country of smoke and fear, where even dreams seemed prohibited and night possessed the complexion of darkness, of the dead. The rubber tree was growing, its leaves seemingly all the more luminous under the rising sun. The trunk sent off shoots and the leaves seemed wide and solidarious palms. Passing by, women spoke to it with words that seemed loving. A very old woman gave it a red sash to drive off the bad luck and perpetual desperation of the city with its generals who also stopped to contemplate the rubber tree, and smile.

The rubber tree was growing in leaps and bounds, looking to climb up along the balconies and the avenues until it began to be bushier and more solidarious than trees themselves. But when it angrily began entering through the door of the general's house, scattering with its shadow the medals hanging in the pavillions, when it razed over the registers of detained prisoners, an order was decreed to lop off its wild and tender branches.

Then, as military men are great believers in their own laws, they came to the fearful conclusion that it would be impossible for them since everything planted in the plaza was decreed a monument of national reconstruction and the rubber tree belonged to the Order of the State, to the pomp of the authorities.

The generals had no choice then but to abandon their uniforms that seemed like dwarf stars, to leave the luxurious trappings of mustard-colored velvet, because the rubber tree had by now entered along the labyrinths of the jails and in the now winged leaves of the rubber tree the hands of the free were raised up and were scaling the walls.

Never was the rubber tree known to slow its growth. Even the very oldest people in the city voicelessly recall the time when the rubber tree, jolted out of the earth, expelled the dictators to the very boundaries of idleness. The rubber tree still continues in the plaza and children sing to it with sounds of love.

LONG LIVE LIFE

LONG LIVE LIFE

I.

And even if my eyes were bandaged and my nose plugged up I would always make my way to her kitchen, to that faithful guardianship of the family meal, to the clay pots and aroma that flowers like light from heaven.

II.

And they speak to her, the old holy witch, her brews in stinking boxes, her little stone treasure trunks where she plants the alchemies of life, where she hides cool leaves of cilantro and a blessed knife shaped from wood. From daybreak, when the mist mixes with her smoky apron, she, the witch, squatting, secret, sweetly cuts the cilantro and with swift fingers sprouts the green, the yellow ones, the tallow silk that resembles moss and life. I watch her on the sly, and her thousand eyes lie in wait for me.

III.

Cilantro is the condiment necessary to breathe, to feel capable of dancing or of death, of reviving and greening anew. As a fairy, she prepares the daily ration in the restless obscurity of early morning. Cilantro wraps around everything and it resembles wheat that sprouts on the palate. While she chops cilantro, she sings or mur-murs and her mouth is a single harvest.

For stomach aches, my wild Mother, who holds us in thrall, boils celery water, then empties it in a black clay pot and it seems as if the water turns green again, it grows, and it goes back under in the black clay, coming up afterwards, floating as at the river's mouth.

In her kitchen there are always percale aprons shaped from ashes, dry banana leaves, slices of potato that she places in a secret pocket, and then suddenly, on the flash of a second, she places all of her belongings on her temples. The toothless lady cures pains and troubles with slices of potato placed on her temples and she closes her eyes the better to hear the noises of things, to hear the scars of the soul.

Garlic surrounded us when I was a girl. Garlic braids for the doorways, for the most unexpected hideaways behind brooms, over the hinges and in the door-bolts. Braids of garlic for love and for cur-ing envy, and now for my son, little goblets of garlic, fragrant, lov-ing, that she piously cradles in his ear, but distant, in her secrets of a poor enchantress.

For love, and love's wrath, she boils little leaves of eucalyp-tus that she chooses herself. Shaping from them a little cross in the left stem she gives them to me so that later she can place them under the bed as an act of faith or show of love.

To ward off sadness, I still search my memory, desperate, for little leaves of eucalyptus to carry in my ravelled pockets, wadded in thread. Then, in the instants when sleep and night absorb us, and life's cracks and crevices come to mind, the odor of eucalyptus slow-ly enters, it begins to hover as if it were a fairy or demon spirit bare-ly suspended from the cracks. Then, I see her approach with her per-cale apron stained by trails of guava, bits of corn caught in her teeth. I see her embrace me, her hands are a crown of cilantro, her aroma is warm, and I slip into her generous width and everything is blue in the room, and all is respendent. Her hands hold me fast, her hands that for me were never those of a servant.

PRAIRIES

It was in the prairies where the immense vastness could be confused with a heaven or an imaginary sea and the immense space of those vast horizons gave out a strange illusion of lost liberty or of absences.

It was a season of luminous autumns. The cone-shaped treetops spread out wide and arched like the bodies of wise witches, like the backs of women, full of fruit in the islands of an interior sea. But we were so far from the sea, although the wind of the plateau could be confused with the fermented bellowing of captive seas.

At times I seemed to myself a wide landscape, forgotten and foreign, and the trees that doubled over with whirling leaves did not let me discern the tenuous luminosity of an anomalous air.

She seemed to follow me around; I also spied on her but protected myself from her goodbyes in the roundness, so sweet and warm, of the trees. Her mouth seemed a great silence in between shadows and her goodbyes produced in me a shuddering sensation between nostalgia and fear.

With a silence that I imagined perverse, she wanted to talk with me and she was always appearing in the roundness, so sweet, of flowering leaves that complained when she went by, sending me a gesture of benevolent silence.

We were destined to an atavistic encounter on the prairies, whose solitude and arid spaces made us all the more venerable and humble.

I always dreamed of her eyes. I dreamed that I secretly fled from her and her blue eyes, immobile, desolate, produced in me an uneasiness in my innermost retreats.

And in the distance of a fatal autumn, we met on a wharf that I dreamed up in my sleep or in a vulgar restaurant called Sunwood. She with a pained, sweet voice asked me where did I get those blue eyes, so very distinct from her own. She assured me that she recognized my wavy hair, my large, imperfect nose. She assured me that she was an expert in genealogy and I only wondered about it because of those strange and fearful blue eyes going back and forth over me, my back gnawing at me with her own sadness and losses.

I told her that my grandfather was from Vienna and that through the love of a cabaret dancer his precious life had been saved. Tearing himself from love he escaped the war and the most perverse holocaust of history. He came to Chile, the blue corner of the planet, and learned the Spanish language, which he loved most of all. He had children and a generous woman named Josephine, name of victorious women.

I told her stories while she, ravenous and sinister, in a learned goodness and a millenary guilt, wanted to know more about my grandfather the Viennese. I told her how his eyes were greener than all springtimes and how my son was named for him, to carry on the tradition of meadows. Then, I could not stop talking to her, and I went back to the story of my great-grandmother, Sonia, the one from Odessa, from shores of salt water seas and dead Jews, and she told me that she too had heard talk of the Jews of Odessa.

I noticed that her skin was beginning to die away or become yellowish and sickly. Meanwhile, she looked at me as if she had seen me forty years before, as if my mouth and my presence were transformed and familiar to her. She tried to look behind my eyes and she saw my naked body, floating with other bodies, she saw me bald while soap was made with my honey-colored skin. She saw men with gilded boots rob me of my young girl's breasts.

And while those exceedingly blue eyes were looking at me in a city full of death and the dead, she wanted me to love her. But she never asked with words, only with a gesture that she made, bending the nape of her neck, and I could see all the sweat of her guilt in her impertinent eyes.

Then, between the regions of madness she told me: "You, too, are an Austrian Jew," and she did not stop looking at me as if with pride and a bit of pity.

I told her that my grandfather loved Vienna, but I preferred the Milky Way to my very small and narrow country called Chile, and in the midst of the silence of the prairies, I asked her what her parents did during that war and what the Viennese did when my grandmother, Elena, resignedly left her books, her sacred candelabra, to walk toward the chambers of terror.

Caught unawares she looked at me. She buried her hands in her hair that was the only thing whirling about in the air in step with the tenuous flame of The Sunwood Inn. With her head lowered she told me and now I can tell it: "My parents worked for the SS in Auschwitz. I saw women burned and being burned with your eyes, with your hair, I saw the blood of Jews who had been set aflame, I saw children being sent off on the death trains, while they played Bach sonatas. Their hair burned as if it were made of rotten wood, and their very blue eyes acquired a tone that was deep but lacking profundity."

Slowly I looked at her and felt a very thin, frozen knife ride over my backbone and I began to choke more with grief for her than for all the naked shoeless women fleeing and in flight towards the gas chambers.

Cornered, she tried to draw closer to me as if she knew that my back was still peopled with the thinnest of needles molded from an atrocious ice and an ice charged with the stories of some deaths far too alive to be erased as forgotten.

And my dead women began to appear in her hair, trying to pardon her and to assure her that lilac-colored loves still exist.

Her blue eyes increasingly began to resemble some Aryan

rivers, some rivers with shabby debris and at times her face would get confused with that face of her parents who paraded in gilt boots through the dreams of my foul-smelling adolescence.

I offered her a glass of white wine like those that they drink in my country to fill up with love, to forget hunger. I offered to be her friend and to take walks along the prairies under the immense cone-shaped treetops. I offered her things that only silence could keep, and she, defenseless, arrogant, asked me to accompany her along the immense groves of poplar trees.

I no longer feared her, but in the vast nights I was liable to see her strangely blue eyes watching for me in the immense space of the horizons, so vast that they give me a strange illusion of freedom from absences.

SARGASSO

María Mercedes isn't from the island. They call her "The Queen" because she goes about dressed in white and in powder. She wears a headband of tiny shell beads. They see her at about eight, when the dew empties out with the sea, the hour when the dead return to the seashores and there she is, once again in the night of mists. I can make her out by the dress that whirls and clambers over the seal-rocks. And she makes as if she were about to dip her feet into the sea, but now she crouches and cradles her toes. Drawing near, crouching low, she looks smaller and smaller, as if she were about to go in. The arch of night lifts and the shameless winds become warmer.

The fog seemed a silhouette waving across the cracks of night, so dusky and full of silence as if all that is deep and dark had joined as one in the very skein of fog over the sea and the night. The sea lay in the distance with a diabolical tranquility and the sand turned upside down in an immense, disorderly, jet black well. No footprints remained on the island. The sandcastles of stupid children lay deformed like the oblique roundness of their heads. They say that they are the children of love between seaweed and the holes left by wrecked ships. With their taciturn errands following the mere semblance of survival, those women so endlessly split and cracked worked all winter long, beating off hunger throughout the marine afternoons. They say they're alone. Dizzy, they begin embroidering in golden wool the apparitions of the virgins of the coasts.

María Mercedes hunches more and more, as if she wanted to enter the water and her body shrinks in front of the immense horizontal line of the water that does not move, that encircles us, that hears us, and the night is so vast and ravenous.

But here she is. What does María Mercedes do before entering the water? Will she know its horrors up close? There's no one on this poisoned beach, not even the demented summer visitors with their cursed phosphorescent suits. There's no one to take her by the hand and to tell her that the water is quite delightful, that it's possible to toss flowers and to baptize the tides. Then, María Mercedes is alone in the absence. Is anything sadder than a woman by seal-rocks? But now, something slips, becomes wet, and her white clothes seem to overflow and mingle with the sky. Many say that the drowned do not fall into the bottom of the sea but rather into the beginning of the sky. Now I am sure that the breaking waves jump out from the sea, that the sea mist is a shattered knife wrapping around her, surrounding her, as if blind, alongside the water, as if complaining, or perhaps snickering on the sly.

María Mercedes appears happy as if she were full of glances and caresses and someone embraces her from behind, entering as if she were made entirely of love, as if she were a seaweed jewel.

Closing in on the water, as if needing no one's help, she walks in. And I imagine her with flowers crowning her—that's why they call her "The Queen"—and I see her so secure with her amber-colored dress, wrapped in what seems like the fog itself and there is no one to stop her or to dry out her body in the sun because María Mercedes walks in. But every time she becomes smaller, night falls, and her wool dress rolls with the density of the scissoring waves or maybe with the shipwrecked face of the sky.

RIVERS

She lay hidden, as if she were the very darkness of night. All night she dreamed of arriving at the roundness of daybreak. Then she enveloped her battered body in wool, winding herself in dusky shawls and she approached the river when the tide seems a quiet death or an empty house of pain's anger. In the village they see her crouch down, her shawl dipped in the water. She cracks open, grey, very dark, her hands become disfigured in the search, as if she were closing up walls and windows, but it is only the terrifying river, the specter of a dry river, like her body bereft of children, plagued by enemy hideouts.

At dawn they also steal from her, watching her all morning long while she kneels, fashioning necklaces from the pebbles heaped up all morning; the wounds in her verdant blood are like the texture of the river. A woman bends searching the coasts for a dead son. Tears fill her, quenching the drought, the otherness, the tears. Beyond words, she wails. Beyond love she seeks out the bone of memory. All night, a woman waits, innocent, for the tides to recede to see if the disfigured bones of her dead son appear, or perhaps a shirt, a shred of clothing, or perhaps a letter of water, something like a sign. She returns empty, they rob her of her glance.

DISTANT ROOT
OF AUTUMN LOVES

I.

All autumn marking the footsteps and the overflowing light brazen and luminous, opening itself up winging its way across the open sky like a wound full of leaves, all autumn at our feet and the roaring of yellow in our mouth, you invite me to make from the trees beds of leaves that are flowers, silence, blankets.

II.

The cloudy river spreading out from our feet like the bright tail of a comet, then my body next to yours growing close as if they were a single drop of water, as if they were the very river that watches us. No one dares throw the first stone and the unclasped hands relax, foreign to combat, they relax taking shelter in that same furrow of water in that same river.

III.

That's how you approach as if to repeat that absence is a empty house but now you're finally ready to fill me with lovely things like toasted bread and the fire will make of me a face that recognizes you even though bandaged.

IV.

Like a long journey hands blaze forth as if they were the lamps, the eyes of god, hands asking things, requesting odors: they want to enter the forest of the body that awaits.

V.

Naked we are so clumsy, fearful, we seem like the children that fashion fortresses and secret hiding places from leaves. Naked after the fortress and the silence. Then I tell you that you grow near in order to disentangle the leaves of love, that all is short and simple, that all is golden like the bodies born from the chimeras of autumn. Then I open up completely like the top of a tree whose shadow summons up the destiny of your hands like a hidden spring of dry leaves.

VI.

Naked you seem like the parks of autumn with the rhapsodies of the Fates, with light filtering out precise and overflowing among the trees. Naked we are two furious and pacified beings returning the gifts of breath, loving one another clandestinely and full of jealousy in the days of autumn in the days of aching whose blankets of yellow are the aged color of desire.

NAKED

I.

you play at stripping me naked, beginning by fastening my hair or it's the wind mixed with the fateful timidity of your hands, drawing close you fall in love with me, your walk becomes a stagger, restless, your desperate hands disobey you, not responding to the consuming immediacy of the body

II.

walking alongside each other, the autumn covers us like the generous wind of days as night or nights as day, happiness brings me closer to the things I love and I feel proud only of what I have loved. Then I look at you to make sure that you have returned, that you are still alive, that absence was only the autumn I did not see in your face or that I felt your desperate, tender hands searching me out before desire turns us into magicians, naked, full of silence. I approach you in the distance of the familiar, in the rituals of the known. You tell me you still lack the courage to join me again, for your body to become translucent in mine. Then tears mingle with time and the word. I do not cry because of what you do or don't say. I cry because of the brevity of being together or because of feeling that I have been betrayed by time.

III.

I cry because of having that chance to take root or to sit down at your table that would be mine.

Nakedness is impossible and clothing hinders love and happiness but in the distances or nearnesses we invent perilous games. Your tongue slips past and joins mine in the knotted vertigo of light. Your hand touches the darkness of my clear legs

I am a village in your speech

whirling, I am a village in your words

becoming naked defies us no longer

in the solitude of the room when the light thrashes at our hair and our threatened eyes we nonetheless remain naked as the room becomes darker and more painful and we're helpless against love and its vertigos and love leaves us speechless and impotent.

HOUSES BY THE SEA

They returned to the house by the sea, looking, out of habit, at the lights on the porches. They lived, day in, day out, without interruptions and without the immense fear of discovering that they loved one another.

Their chief entertainment consisted of looking at the blue of the sea in the full nights when they were naked, so that in the shadow they seemed newly immobile, like the statues of lost transients. But there they were, like night itself, playing infinite palpitations and the sound of the water wiped away their names and their ages.

She is a young woman with the wind by the sea. She has left the colored stockings, the uniforms, the polished nails of chubby hands. It is the beginning of summer and she abandons the terraces of the great hotels to strip naked with the smell of the sea in the mouth of the old man, to become an apple tree in the immense, fearful, winged marine night.

All night the bodies love each other, they play at wandering and he regals the ear with obscene, delirious, gloomy words. Then, for the first time, she fears the perverse lover. She begs him not to go on with those vulgarities in her girl's breast. But the old man tells her that it is impossible to stop loving her so, like ferocious wolves in a bloody night of forests and sperm.

They step out on the balcony and gaze off at the blue of the coasts. Dogs wander along the beach and they hear the shuffle of drunken footsteps. The silence dances like a swift knife, much like passion, like nights of love in the house by the rocks, in the houses by the sea. And she sees how he begins to separate from her body but since they are alone and naked she lets him make of her a crashing of water, a symphony of mortal blood between the sheets.

THE DREAMS OF VAN GOGH

All yellow like the threads of wild braids, all sun like in the wells of time. Then I learned of the travelling painter with his easel slung over his shoulder, casting light on pilgrimages, on wild paths, on the traces of water below the shadows and the fields.

In Arles, in St. Rémy he searches, looking for himself. Debilitated, he relies on distance, he buries his hand in the mossy rotund thickness of his soul and of earth, he pulls out all the green, the grasses, the beginnings of odor. Then, maddened by the crackling beauty, he makes it all the more ours, he begins to paint, choosing life.

Everything catches his glance, but soon, on the canvas by his side, immense, he lets it go free, fresh, agile. He begins with the details, he lashes his easel to the wind. Wandering through Arles, he wastes himself in space. They try to lock him up but he becomes the very dream of sunflowers.

Furious, he returns to the path of the helpless, to the strange, vertiginous blue of the night. He portrays those who, deep below the earth, are waiting, who are rebuilding life. He paints potatos and the poor, all asleep with deep color, he paints fire and the dailiness of life.

The traveling painter sits down in a blue chair. Everything is spinning around, encircling his crooked hairs. He paints the air and leaves it.